NURSE IN CLOVER

After she had suffered heartbreak, Nurse
Ann Bowman returned to Yorkshire from
the Caribbean to work at Clover House,
a nursing home owned by her parents.
When she met the other doctor at the
nursing home, Barry Lander, she sensed
he was going to play an important part
in her life. Her old friends, Petra Graham
and Hugh Leighton were also destined to
have a great influence upon her future and
soon Ann was looking forward to making
a success of her new life, hoping that this
time her romantic plans would succeed.

NURSE IN CLOVER

Nurse In Clover

by
Donna Rix

Dales Large Print Books
Long Preston, North Yorkshire,
England.

British Library Cataloguing in Publication Data.

Rix, Donna
    Nurse in clover.

A catalogue record for this book is
available from the British Library

ISBN 1-85389-870-8 pbk

First published in Great Britain by Robert Hale & Company,
1973

Copyright © 1973 by Donna Rix

Cover illustration © Len Thurston by arrangement with
P.W.A. International Ltd.

The moral right of the author has been asserted

Published in Large Print 1998 by arrangement with Robert
Hale Ltd.

Dales Large Print is an imprint of
Library Magna Books Ltd.
Printed and bound in Great Britain by
T.J. International Ltd., Cornwall, PL28 8RW.

Chapter One

Ann Bowman still hadn't quite recovered from the shock of her sudden decision to leave the Caribbean and come home to Yorkshire to Clover House Nursing Home in the little village of Clover in the east of the county. When she thought about it she still marvelled that she had decided to leave Gerry once and for all before she had married him. Now the taxi was taking her on the last lap of her long journey and she was trying to straighten out her thoughts and wonder about the future. She had to get her story right for her parents, and she didn't plan to tell them the whole truth about her life in the sunshine across the world.

A sigh escaped her as they passed through the village of Clover, and a smile touched her lips when she recalled the last time she had seen it. That was three years before when Gerry had taken her away to a life which she had expected to be filled with excitement and adventure and love.

She glossed over the disillusionment which had followed, and a sigh of relief passed her lips as she told herself yet again that she had done the right thing. Gerry never intended to marry her!

She didn't feel bitter about it! At first she had been hurt. But the process of realization had been so long-drawn that she was aware of the situation subconsciously before it really came home to her.

Ann stiffened herself as the taxi turned into the driveway of Clover House, and she smiled as she glanced at the large white board bearing the legend: *Nursing Home*. It seemed as if nothing had changed here in the past three years, and for a moment nostalgia touched her inside and she cringed against the hurt that lay covered in her heart. But she wouldn't open any graves, she told herself firmly. She had cut her losses and she was well out of it.

The taxi stopped in front of the large, four storey house, and Ann sat staring up at it from the window of the vehicle while her mind flashed with pictures from memory. Her parents operated this place, her father a doctor and her mother a nursing Sister before she became the Matron here. Clover house had been the Bowman family seat for generations, and beyond the house lay Clover Farm, which was run by her uncle, Charles Bowman.

'We've arrived, Miss,' the driver said, breaking in upon her thoughts. 'I'll put your luggage on the steps, shall I?'

'Yes, please, Driver!' Ann opened the car door and alighted, taking up her smallest case and her handbag, and her brown eyes gleamed as she studied the entrance to Clover House. She had lived in the house before it had been a Nursing Home. She had been born here, and brought up here, and now she had returned because she needed to think about her future and what it might hold.

The door of the house opened as she paid off the driver, and Ann mounted the six steps towards her mother. Mrs Bowman was fifty-three, a graceful woman whose black hair showed no signs of age. She was smiling now as she came towards Ann, who held out her arms, and they embraced warmly.

'Mother! It's wonderful to see you again!'

'Ann! I haven't got over the shock of your telegram.' Mrs Bowman pushed

9

Ann to arm's length and looked into her daughter's brown eyes. 'What on earth happened to make you leave there so precipitously?'

'You know me, Mother!' Ann spoke jocularly, smiling and trying to appear unconcerned. 'I suddenly thought I'd like to live in England again, so here I am.'

'And what about Gerry?' Mrs Bowman studied Ann's oval face, taking in the deep tan that was a legacy of three years living under tropic conditions. There were shadows in Ann's dark eyes which she could not conceal, and Ann looked away quickly, afraid that she might have to tell the truth.

'How is Father?' she demanded.

'He's fine, and just dying to see you. He had to go out today, of all days! But he'll be back this evening. Come on in and I'll get Douglas to take your bags to your room. It's wonderful to see you again, Ann. You've grown up a great deal in the past three years! It's amazing how time flies. But the days dragged at times when I used to think of you all those thousands of miles away.'

'I'm home for good now,' Ann said. She slipped her arm through her mother's

10

and they walked up the remaining steps to the entrance. 'I don't know what to do with myself, but I look forward to nursing again.'

A porter wearing a long white coat came hurrying forward, and Mrs Bowman gave him instructions regarding Ann's luggage. Ann was looking around with interest, and the scene that greeted her was the same one she remembered leaving. Nothing seemed to have changed.

'Is Sister Harmer still with you, Mother?' she demanded.

'Yes, but she's Assistant Matron now,' came the steady reply. 'Nurse Corbin was promoted to Sister, and so was Nurse Tamworth. You knew them both very well. Nurse Pierce is still with us, and so is Nurse Williams. But you won't know Nurse Dermot. She joined us last year.'

'And Doctor Hookham?' Ann queried.

'He left us last year—went to Canada. We have a Doctor Lander with us now. You'll like him, Ann. He's thirty-one and a really nice person. I've been a bit worried about him lately, but I'll tell you all about him later. Right now I want to know what you've been doing with yourself these past three years. I scent a mystery in your past,

11

and I want to get to the very bottom of it.'

'There's nothing to tell,' Ann said slowly as they walked to the private wing of the house. 'Do I get my old room back?'

'Of course you do! And there's a job here for you if you want it.'

'Thank you, Mother.' Ann paused for a moment and looked into her mother's steady eyes. 'I'll tell you all about Gerry later, I promise.'

'There's plenty of time. Now you're back with us you must give yourself a break and take things easy. You have plenty of time. I want your company a great deal in the next week or two. I've missed you terribly during the last three years.'

'I'm sorry I ever went away, Mother!' Ann smiled, but there was a hardness in her eyes for a moment, and Mrs Bowman saw it. 'It's like a miracle being back. This time last week I didn't know I'd be making the decision. Now here I am!'

They went on into the private wing through a doorway that cut across the ground floor corridor, and Mrs Bowman hooked back the door for the porter to get through with Ann's luggage.

'I see you've had the place decorated in

my absence,' Ann commented.

'Your room is just as you left it,' her mother replied. 'We are not touched by time in this place, except for ourselves, of course. I expect you can see the difference in me now, can't you?'

'I was just thinking that you're wearing pretty well considering your age,' Ann said, chuckling.

'You've changed considerably!' Mrs Bowman looked into Ann's eyes. 'You're hiding misery, Ann, aren't you?'

'I never could conceal anything from you, could I?' Ann countered. 'But it isn't misery, Mother. I think I'm more concerned about three wasted years than anything else.'

'So you have broken with Gerry!'

'Oh yes! He's staying on out there and I shall never go back.' For a moment Ann was sharp eyed, and her lips trembled. Then she drew a sharp breath and let it go slowly. 'He decided that he did not want marriage within the next five years, and I decided that I didn't want to marry him at all. It's as simple as that, Mother. I haven't come running home to you because things didn't work out. I just wanted to come home and try again.'

'Was Gerry beastly to you?'

'No!' Ann smiled slowly. 'It was rather the other way. He never had any time for me! Everything and everyone came before me.'

'And you stuck it for three years?'

'Well, I didn't want you or father thinking that I hadn't given it a good try.'

'You know us better than that,' Mrs Bowman said.

'I know that I was supposed to be going over there to make a wonderful new life!' Ann said wryly. 'I left a lot of friends behind who are going to ask questions when we meet again.'

'You may not find so many of them around now. A lot of changes have taken place in the neighbourhood. It's only Clover House that remains the same.'

'Yes, I suppose some of the girls have married, and no doubt some of the old gang have moved away. Life doesn't stand still for anyone.' Ann's voice quivered, and she shook her head slowly as they mounted the stairs to where her old room was situated. 'I like this wallpaper,' she declared when her mother opened the door of her room for her.

'I had it done last year. When you wrote saying you might be coming home for a month's holiday. But that never took place, did it. What exactly happened?'

'I thought perhaps I might need some money in reserve, so I saved it,' Ann said with a thin smile.

The porter had followed them up the stairs, and they stepped aside for the luggage to be deposited in the room. Ann looked at the man's tall figure. He was a stranger to her. She glanced at her mother, who smiled.

'You don't know Douglas Shenton, Ann. He started after you went away. Douglas, this is my daughter, Ann. I'm sure you've heard us talking about her.'

'Yes, Matron.' He nodded, his pale eyes gleaming. 'How do you do, Miss Bowman? I expect it's a lot hotter where you've just come from.'

'It is,' Ann agreed, glancing towards the window, and she had to stifle a shiver. This was the end of September, and she had felt the difference in the atmosphere from the moment she stepped off the airliner at London Airport. 'I shall need some thick clothes now.'

Shenton smiled and departed, and Ann

15

looked around the room.

'You'll find some of your old clothes still hanging in your wardrobe, but I doubt if any of them will fit you now. Three years is a changeable period for a girl of your age.' Mrs Bowman nodded knowingly, and Ann mentally agreed.

'Let's forget about me for a bit, Mother,' she said. 'I want to know what's been happening around here while I've been away. I remember you writing to say that some alterations had been made, some extensions added. How many patients do you have at this time?'

'Fifty-seven at the moment, but our capacity is seventy-five. We haven't the staff to deal with that number, but if you join us and we get another nurse as well we could build up to our maximum.'

'This place has been a great success, hasn't it?'

'Better than your father ever imagined. He couldn't have done anything better with Clover House when your grandfather died. It was a good arrangement your father and your Uncle Charles made. Uncle Charles runs the farm and your father has this place. It's everything to him, you know. He'd never take any time off if I didn't insist.'

'And what about you, Mother?' Ann looked into Mrs Bowman's face. 'Are you happy?'

'I couldn't be happier! You know that nursing has always been my whole life, and I wouldn't want to change a single thing from the way it is now. Of course I was concerned about you, being on the other side of the world. But now you're home and you're going to stay. I'm happy now, Ann, without reservation.'

Ann smiled and went to her mother's side, putting her arms around the older woman's neck. 'I've missed you too,' she admitted. 'I would have come home before this if I hadn't been afraid of what people might say. But I decided to give it three years, and no one can say that I didn't give it a good try.'

'So you've been very unhappy out there!'

'Not really. Disillusioned is a better word. But dreams are made to be tumbled, aren't they? It happens all the time in this world. I have no regrets, I suppose. I've seen something of the world, and I took care of myself. I proved I could do it. But now I'm back and I'm glad to be here.'

'You must be tired after your long trip.' Mrs Bowman held Ann's hands for a moment, and looked into her daughter's liquid brown eyes. 'Why don't you relax for a bit! You'll need to change. I've got some things to do, but I'll have time to sit with you later. We have a lot to talk about, and no doubt you'll think of a great number of questions to ask. It's wonderful having you back home again, Ann, and I want to have your company a lot in coming days to make up for the time we've lost.'

'I want the same thing, Mother!' Ann felt a wave of emotion sweep through her and she hugged her mother and kissed her cheek. 'The times I've wished I could see your dear face! It's like a dream, now, looking at you in the flesh. But don't let me keep you from your duties. A Nurse's work is never done!'

'We both know that! But if you decide to nurse here with us you'll find it different to working in a hospital.'

'I've got a lot of thinking to do before I decide upon the course of my future,' Ann said.

'Does that mean you might be leaving us again?'

Ann shook her head. 'I don't think so! I don't want to go away from home again!'

'That's a relief to know!' Mrs Bowman

hugged Ann and then moved away. 'Make yourself at home. You know where everything is.'

Ann went to the window after her mother had departed, and she stood watching the grounds while her thoughts roamed free through the past. She had grown up here at Clover House, and she realized now that all the time she had been away her heart had been here. She sighed heavily, but filled with satisfaction, and then she turned away and jerked herself from her thoughts. She began to unpack, and there was a not a sad or wistful thought in her head.

By the time she had settled back into her room Ann was feeling hungry, and a glance at her watch showed the time to be just after twelve-thirty. She searched through the clothes which she had left behind when she went abroad, and found a thick tweed skirt, and a heavy woollen jumper, which she donned. Sitting at her dressing table, she looked at her reflection and examined her face critically. There were faint lines at the corners of her eyes which could soon turn into crowsfeet, she thought. She smiled, watching her lips curve richly as she did so. Where was the young girl with the high ideals now? The question touched

19

her mind and started her off thinking in a totally different direction ...

But thinking wasn't going to help her at all, she thought, and returned her attention to examining her features. Her long black hair framed her oval face, helping to conceal the long line of her nose. She firmed her lips, then reached for her make-up and began to repair the damages of travel. She was sparing in her use of make-up. She had never done anything in excess! She smiled at the thought and got up to go and find her mother.

Ann had lunch with her mother, and afterwards decided to take a walk around the Home. Mrs Bowman was too busy to accompany her, but Ann felt the need to be alone, to let her mind adjust to this homecoming without pressures from anyone influencing her in any way.

'I think I'll walk over to the farm,' she said as they arose from the lunch table. 'Uncle Charles is all right, is he?'

'Yes, and he still comes over on Friday evenings,' Mrs Bowman replied with a smile. 'I told him you were coming home and he was excited about it. You were always his favourite niece.'

'That's understandable, seeing that I'm his only niece!' Ann retorted. 'What about Paul? How is he these days?' She frowned a little as she remembered the last scandal before she left which had surrounded her cousin. Paul Bowman had always been a wilful type, unmindful of his father's prominent position in the highest social circles of the area. Aunt Beth had died while Paul had been small, and he had never known the influence of a female. She could remember that as a boy Paul had been a constant source of trouble to his father and the Bowman name.

'Paul has settled down a great deal since you've been away, Ann. He did have that last lot of trouble, which was cleared up before you went, but since then we've heard very little of his doings. In fact we haven't seen much of him. He went to Agricultural College and passed with honours, but I'd say his heart is not set on the farm.'

'I always said he wouldn't make a farmer,' Ann said. She was remembering the times Paul had come to the House for the day. They had never got along particularly well, and most visits ended in fighting between them. 'I'll walk across there this afternoon and see if can I find Uncle.'

She felt a desire to get out and look at all the old familiar places, and as soon as she was ready, dressed in her thicker clothes and wearing a russet coat and heavy shoes, she set out along the path at the rear of the building which led to the back gate.

The grass wet her shoes instantly, and Ann went on with a cheerfulness born of novelty. It had been a long time since she'd been able to walk in wet grass. The whole atmosphere was damp, and water dripped from the trees. Most of the branches were shedding their leaves, and the ground was littered with them. They rustled wetly as Ann dragged her feet through them like a child, and she laughed with pure relief and pleasure.

She departed by the back gate and walked along the path that led to the distant farm buildings clustered behind the square farmhouse. She paused on a rise in the ground and looked at the house, picturing her Uncle Charles. He was so like her father that they were often mistaken for twins, although there was a space of four years between their ages; Uncle Charles being the older. She went on again after some minutes of musing about the past, and her eyes spotted many familiar landmarks which she had forgotten about. Then she came to the kissing gate, and she paused some yards from it and studied it as if she had never seen it before. But her mind was sending pictures of the past into her consciousness, and she remembered the last time she'd looked at this scene.

It had been on her holiday here with Gerry before they'd left England three years before. They'd spent a wonderful fortnight in June, just wandering around without a care, feeling very much in love and being on top of the world.

Ann smiled wryly at the recollections. Well that was one great dream which had come to naught. She shook herself mentally and went on, pushing through the gateway, the iron gate creaking as it turned on rusty hinges, and even the squeaking seemed to sound exactly the same as it had done years before. She found her mind clouding over with nostalgia, and she tried vainly to clear it.

Then she came upon the brook, with the small rustic bridge crossing it, and she leaned on the wooden rail and glanced down into the bubbling water, seeing her reflection as she had done so many times in the past, and she wondered how much water had flowed under the bridge since she was last here. She was older and wiser now; at least, she hoped she was wiser.

She fell to musing, and time passed her by. The sound of the water was soothing, giving her just the right background for her thoughts, and her reflection wavered on the uneasy surface of the stream. She saw minnows darting hither and thither in the ruffled water and it seemed to her that it was only yesterday when she used to come fishing here with her cousin Paul, although he invariably managed to push her in before their day ended.

With a sigh she pushed herself erect and prepared to go on, but a voice startled her and she glanced around quickly, fully expecting to see Paul coming towards her with a jar and a long handled net. But she saw instead a stranger seated on a camp stool, and easel and canvas before him. He was peering at her from around the side of the canvas.

'Please don't move for a moment,' he called. 'You've been standing there five minutes without moving, so I've put you into the picture. You're exactly what I need to give the scene a point of interest, and your posture was so natural. You were miles away and standing exactly right.'

'Oh!' Ann was so surprised that she felt he must have been reading her thoughts while she had been unaware of him. She felt slightly confused for a moment, and didn't know whether to hurry away. Then her natural friendliness asserted itself and she smiled. 'Exactly how was I standing?' she demanded.

'Leaning on the rail with one elbow and that faraway expression on your face.' He had a shock of fair hair hanging over his forehead, and his smiling face seemed to convey vibrant animation.

Ann resumed her former position, glancing at him to see if her attitude was right, and he nodded emphatically.

'That's it perfectly. Now if you wouldn't mind holding it for a few minutes I'll capture you exactly.'

He was only yards away, and Ann wondered why she hadn't spotted him in the first place. But she had been so engrossed in her thoughts that her surroundings had entirely escaped her.

'Only a few more moments,' he encouraged. 'Nearly finished now. I didn't really like to announce my presence when I saw you standing there. You were so completely unaware of your surroundings! You fitted the scene perfectly.'

Ann glanced up at the sky, which was beginning to threaten rain. 'Isn't this the wrong time of year to be painting outdoors?' she demanded.

'Not at all. I like Autumn scenes. The shades and colours are beautiful. I'm Barry Lander, by the way. I'm the doctor at the Nursing Home behind you. Do you live around here?' He paused, but went on again before Ann could reply. 'There! That does it! I've got you in as I want you. I can add the details later.' He was smiling as Ann turned towards him again. 'I'll remember your colouring. Long black hair and brown eyes! An Autumn rose, I should say!'

'There isn't such a thing,' she retorted, walking towards him.

'There is now!' He got to his feet and towered over her, looking down into her face with sharp blue eyes. There was a smear of brown paint on his left cheek, and his long fingers were liberally daubed with various colours. There was even paint on his dark tweed jacket, and he didn't seem at all like a doctor to Ann. She guessed that he was about thirty, and he had pleasant features that made her feel friendly towards him although she never made a habit of instant friendship.

'So you're Doctor Lander!' She said when they stood facing one another.

'And you're Ann Bowman!' He smiled gravely. 'How do you do? Are you pleased to be home?'

'How do you know me?' she asked, more than a little surprised.

'Your photograph stands on the sideboard in your mother's lounge. I've looked at it a great many times in the year or so that I've been here, and of course your mother talked about you every time I had tea with her.'

'Oh!' A smile broke the puzzlement on her face, and Ann nodded. 'So you knew me the moment you saw me!'

'Not immediately. I watched you for some time before realising who you are.'

'May I see your painting?' She began to move around him.

'Certainly. I'm not very good. But I like painting, and I do it as a relaxation more

27

than anything else.'

She looked at the scene, nodding slowly. 'It is good,' she commented. 'It's very good. You've captured the bridge and the surrounding scenery quite well. But I think I spoil the picture. The bridge ought to be left empty.'

'I'll put you in, and I can always blot you out when it's finished if I don't like you!'

She looked into his blue eyes and smiled. 'I'm not a very likeable person,' she said.

'Well you look likeable, and if you have inherited the temperaments of your parents then you ought to be nice to know.'

Ann smiled, and she liked the way he talked. He seemed a very nice person himself, and suddenly she felt a twinge of intuition. She had always believed that Fate took a hand in life, although its interference was never readily apparent. But as she looked at Barry Lander she sensed that this meeting with him would prove to be a milestone in her life. It was uncanny how the impression clung to her mind. She caught her breath and tried to break the thought. But she felt like a fly caught on sticky paper, and suddenly she was not in full command of her wits. He

28

spoke to her and she answered as if in a dream. There was an intangible power about him which enveloped her like an invisible fog.

She became so confused that she made some hurried excuse and departed from him, leaving him to collect together his impedimenta, and she hurried on to the farm, glancing back from time to time as if afraid that Doctor Lander was pursuing her. She was quite shaken by the experience.

Chapter Two

Ann went on to Clover Farm, and she was breathless by the time she reached the big house. She hadn't been hurrying, but her shoulders were heaving and she felt stifled. Even now she glanced back to see where Doctor Lander had got to, but he was not in view, and she moistened her suddenly dry lips as she thought about him.

However her thoughts glossed over the meeting when she saw her uncle. Charles Bowman was standing in the drive talking with a stranger who stood by a gleaming American car, and for a moment Ann thought she was staring at her father instead of her uncle; they were so much alike.

'Ann!' He broke off his conversation and came hurrying towards her. 'So you've arrived at last! I was pleased when I heard you were coming home.' He seized her hand and pumped it vigorously. 'Those foreign places are not for you. This is where you belong. Welcome back home!'

'Thank you, Uncle,' she said happily. 'It's very nice to be home again.'

They stepped aside as the man her uncle had been talking to began to drive away, and Charles Bowman lifted a hand in farewell.

'That's one of the Ministry men,' Charles said, his dark eyes narrowing for a moment. 'I'm having some trouble getting planning permission for a house to be built on a plot near the main road. Paul is thinking of getting married at last and he wants to live on the farm but not in my house.'

'How is Paul these days?' Ann enquired.

'He's settled down a lot, and he's been working steadily around here. It's more than I ever hoped for, I can tell you, Ann.' Charles linked his arm through Ann's and they began to walk towards the house. 'But tell me about yourself. Are you home for good? Why didn't you marry that doctor you went away with three years ago?'

'I am home for good, and I didn't marry because marriage would have interfered with his plans. Gerry was always filled with big ideas, and he had no time for me.' She smiled up at him. He had always been like a second father to her, and they were very good friends. 'What's been happening

32

around the farm while I've been away?'

'Nothing has changed much, except me,' he retorted, scratching his chin. 'We've expanded a bit, ploughed in more grassland, but it's a struggle to show any fair profit. Times haven't improved for farmers, I can tell you.' He smiled wryly. 'I always did say your father had more brains than me, and he's certainly proved it with the Nursing Home. I never thought he'd make a success of the venture, but he's proved me wrong, and he's still going ahead.'

'I haven't seen him yet. He's away today. Is Paul around?'

'He's somewhere about the farm, but I can never tell you where. He'll be pleased to see you. You were both very friendly when you were children.'

'That's because we had no one else to play with,' she declared. 'I might have been a bit of a tomboy in my childhood, but Paul always gave me a hard time of it. I was down at the brook just now, and I couldn't remember the number of times Paul pushed me into the water.'

Charles Bowman laughed heartily, and Ann smiled as she shook her head. But mentioning the brook brought Barry

Lander back to mind, and she narrowed her eyes as she recalled his tall figure and pleasant face. His blue eyes had seemed to bore right through her, and she felt her pulses race as she considered what had passed between them. There was a sudden itch in her mind, informing her that she was getting impatient to see him again, and she wondered about him, unable to understand what it was about him that seemed to tug at her instincts and subconsciousness.

'I'm sorry, Uncle, but what were you saying?' she said, dragging her thoughts back to the present.

'Do you have any regrets about coming home?' he repeated, eyeing her shrewdly.

'None at all! I've been wanting to come home for some time.'

'I may be old fashioned, but I believe a person should stay in the area where he's born.'

'You say that because you have so much here!' Ann smiled. 'I liked the tropical weather. It suited me fine. There was swimming whenever I felt like it, and you've only got to look at me to see I did a lot of sunbathing.'

'It's all right if you're a millionaire

and don't have to work for a living,' he protested. 'But where would I find the time for that sort of thing?'

'You'd look cute in a Panama hat and Bermuda shorts,' she said.

He chuckled, and they entered the house. 'Would you like something to drink?' he asked.

'No thanks!' She shook her head. 'I don't drink anything but limejuice.'

'That will make you sour, surely! We'll have to have a get together to celebrate your homecoming. Tell your mother I'll bring Paul over one evening. He wants you all to meet his future wife.'

'I'll get mother to telephone you. I don't know what her duties are, and Father always seemed to be on duty before I went away. I don't suppose he's changed at all in the past three years.'

'Three years is not a long time,' Charles said, his dark eyes gleaming.

'It seems to have been a good slice out of my life,' she retorted.

She stayed with her uncle for almost an hour, hoping that Paul would show up, but in the end she decided to go around the farm looking for her cousin. She left Charles in his study, where he was working on his accounts, and set out to look over the buildings.

Recollections of her childhood returned as she went through the yards and peered into the various erections. But she found some new piggeries and fowl houses, and several new barns had been added to the cluster that was Clover Farm.

Then Paul appeared, emerging from a barn, and he paused in some surprise at sight of her, until he recognized her. Then he came forward with a huge grin on his face, and he seized hold of her and lifted her feet from the ground, swinging her around until they were both dizzy.

'Ann!' he declared when he finally set her feet back on the ground. 'It's great to see you again. I was pleased when I heard you were coming home. Three years! Time has flown.'

'It hasn't for me,' she retorted, looking into his tanned face. His dark eyes were bright and glinting. 'But I must say you're looking very well, Paul! How are you doing?'

'Fine, just fine! I'm planning on getting married in about six months. I'm glad you're home so you'll be able to come to the wedding. But there were no wedding bells for you, I understand. What went wrong? If you remember, I told you once that I didn't think you'd ever get Gerry to marry you.'

'So you did,' she said softly. 'I wouldn't hear of it, remember?'

'I remember only too well. But now you're home you can look over the field again and find someone who suits you.'

'Are there any of the old gang still around?' she demanded.

'Some are, but I don't get around much anymore.' He chuckled. 'Penelope won't let me off the chain, and truth to tell, I wouldn't want to go out without her now.'

'Well you have changed. I'd certainly like to meet Penelope. She must be quite a girl if she's made you toe the line.'

'I didn't think the girl was born who could lead me around by the nose,' he agreed.

Ann studied him. He seemed to have filled out considerably in the past three years. His face was fleshy, and he seemed to be happy. She was remembering that in the past he was morose at times. But a girl in his life would make all the difference, and she was pleased that he had found someone.

'What are you going to do now you're home?' he asked.

'I need a holiday first,' she replied. 'But I expect I'll work as a nurse at the Home. Mother has told me there's a position there for me. I don't think I shall be going off again.'

'I'm glad to hear it. I've missed you, Ann.'

'I've often thought about you!' She looked into his eyes for a moment, and inexplicably, Barry Lander's face seemed to swim in her mind. She blinked and firmed her lips. 'It's nice to be home,' she went on. 'There were several times when I thought about making the break, but something always prevented it. But now I'm here and I have the feeling that I'll never want to leave home again.'

'Were you unhappy out there then?'

'Not with the place. It's marvellous. The weather is out of this world, and working at the hospital never seemed half as much work as working here in England. But that was only the half of it. I'm going to settle down here and work as hard as I possibly can.'

'Well don't do it all. Leave something for the others. You won't be very popular if you start working at the Home and showing all the other nurses up, will you?'

Ann smiled. She glanced at her watch. 'Well I'll set a good pace,' she retorted, 'I suppose I'd better be going back. It gets dark fairly early at this time of the year, doesn't it?'

'You've got plenty of time. Will you come over one evening? I'd like you to meet Penelope.'

'I don't know her from way back?'

'I don't think so! Her family moved into the old Howard farm about two years ago. They come from Sussex. Penelope's father is a retired Colonel.'

'Oh!' Ann pulled a face at him. 'No wonder you're toeing the line these days.'

'Well it's about time I settled down,' he said with a grin. 'I must say you're looking even lovelier than ever. What was wrong with Gerry? Did he go blind, or something?'

'Gerry wasn't blind, so whatever happened comes under the or something,' she retorted. A sigh gusted through her but she fought it and controlled it. 'It's nice seeing you again, Paul. We'll make arrangements about coming over, or you're coming across to the Home, I believe. Mother will telephone. Now I'll let you get on with your work and I'll go back.'

'Thanks for coming. I was wondering when you would arrive. No one seemed to know for certain. I'll pass the word round among some of our friends to let them know you're back. You can expect a call or two as soon as they hear.'

'It will be a pleasure! Goodbye, Paul.'

'Goodbye, and you'd better hurry if you're taking the footpath. It's going to rain.'

She lifted a hand in acknowledgement as she started away, and her thoughts were fleeting as she left the farm and started for home. When she reached the brook she looked around eagerly for signs of Barry Lander, but he had gone, and she stood for a moment on the little bridge and thought about him.

A spot of rain struck her forehead, and another touched her nose. She sighed as she dragged herself from her reverie, and she went on along the path, making for the Home which showed its red roof among the tall trees surrounding it. The wind began to howl dismally and rain came down in a sudden shower, soaking her instantly. Her heavy coat became sodden, but she kept walking steadily, enjoying the wetness and the coldness of it. She had missed this for three years. This was the first time she'd been in an English downpour since leaving all those months and months ago.

Her feet slipped and slithered on the muddy path, and fallen leaves didn't help any. But she smiled to herself and walked in a brisk manner, ignoring the fact that cold streams of water were trickling down her neck and that her long black hair was being plastered to her head. She kept her face tilted towards the ground to avoid the worst of the rain, and plodded on up a steep rise that had her breathless before she reached the crest.

'I say!' The voice cut at her, destroying her sense of loneliness and startling her for a moment.

Ann looked round quickly, and saw Barry Lander standing under a big oak, sheltering from the weather, his easel and canvas protected by his raincoat. He looked as if he had been caught in the downpour, and he was smiling at her as she stood unmindful in the rain.

'Oh hello!' She went towards him,

smiling. 'Your painting hasn't got wet, has it?'

'No, it's quite well protected. But what about you? You were striding along there as if the sun were shining. Were your thoughts so far away that you didn't realise it was raining?'

'I'm not that bad,' she retorted lightly. 'I did actually notice the rain. But I promised myself when I was out there in all that heat that when I came home I'd stand out in the first shower of rain.' She smiled. 'So here I am!'

He nodded understandingly, and there was a grin on his face.

'A promise is a promise,' he said. 'You don't believe in doing things by halves, do you? I shouldn't think there's a dry stitch on you.'

'Clothes will dry,' she retorted. Now she was looking at him intently, trying to discover what it was that had attracted her to him in the first instant. But there was nothing tangible about him, nothing she could point at as being the cause for it all. She began to realise that she was getting breathless again, and she was merely standing before him. 'I suppose you stayed too long at the brook,' she went on.

'There's never enough perfect daylight these days,' he replied. 'I did notice rain coming up, but I forgot about it when you happened along.' He moved further under the tree. 'Perhaps you'd better join me here for a few moments, at least until it eases a little.'

She moved to his side and pushed quite close to him, looking up into his face, and he was smiling easily although he didn't meet her eyes. He was rather handsome, she told herself. His blue eyes were honest and warm, and she always judged a man by his eyes. She listened for a moment to the rain beating down around them, and as the drops came down through the branches they made tiny swishing sounds. The air was quite damp and most refreshing.

'You're enjoying every minute of this, aren't you?' he asked, and she looked up at him.

'Very much so! I wouldn't care if I had to stand here for the rest of the day.'

'Well I have to go on duty.' He glanced at his watch and nodded to himself. 'Perhaps I shouldn't have come out this afternoon with your father away for the day. But he insisted that I took my time off.'

'Do you like being here at Clover House?'

'Very much! I've never been happier. It's a very comfortable place.'

'It's rather lonely. I know because I lived here most of my life.' She smiled. 'The Bowman family have lived here for several generations. But it looks as if I'm the last one in our particular branch of the family. Have you met my cousin Paul?'

'Yes. I've seen quite a lot of him since I've been here. I think he's a nice person.' His tones were gentle, and Ann took the opportunity to study him while he glanced away across the fields into the driving rain.

'We're going to be stuck here for some time by the looks of it,' she said cheerfully.

'You wouldn't get any wetter if you walked the rest of the way in it,' he responded.

'Thank you. You're quick in your judgements. You only met me this afternoon and already you're voicing an opinion of my mental state.'

'I didn't mean it that way!' He glanced at her, a little startled, and then he saw that she was smiling, and he chuckled.

Ann liked the way he accepted her leg-pulling, and she warmed to him still more.

44

She began to wonder about him. Where had he come from? What had happened in his life before his arrival here? She broke off her thoughts when she saw that he was looking at her rather closely, and as their glances met he smiled.

'I can't help feeling that I know you quite well,' he said. 'Your mother has talked so much about you that I've formed a mental picture of you in my mind, and I'm trying to match up what I'm seeing now with what I thought I knew.'

'That's fatal for me, I expect,' Ann said lightly. 'But mothers do talk a lot about their only daughters, you know.'

'I'm sure nothing was exaggerated in your case.'

'That sounds ominous. What did Mother make me out to be? I suspect, judging by your expression, that you've gained the impression I'm not quite right in the head.'

'Well you were strolling along in the pouring rain as if the sun was shining high overhead,' he suggested.

Ann laughed, liking his tones and his manner. 'That doesn't sound any more crazier than painting outside in Autumn,' she reported.

45

'I wouldn't have got you on the bridge if I hadn't been there today.' He nodded. 'I don't care what you think of me, but I have perfected the composition of my picture, thanks to you, and that's all I wanted today.'

'A satisfied man! One has to travel a long way today to find such a spectacle.'

'You've got a poor outlook on the world in general and men in particular. I hope your words don't conceal bitterness at some harsh treatment you've received at the hands of some unscrupulous man.'

'No!' She sighed as she spoke. 'No doubt Mother has told you all about me, about Gerry and the reasons we went to the Caribbean in the first place.'

'Yes, she did give me quite a bit of the story. I gather things didn't work out too well for you. I'm sorry. But you don't look too upset by what's happened, if I may take the liberty of saying so.'

'No.' Ann shook her head slowly. 'I'm not upset at all. It was something that just didn't work out.'

'I suppose you know most of the staff at the Home here.' He changed the subject adroitly.

'I do! Most of them have been with

Father for a long time.'

'It's quite a nice place. I've been here a year now, and I wouldn't want to leave to go anywhere else. I tried a number of places before settling here.'

'Where is your home?' Ann asked.

'In London—Wimbledon. But I'm in exile here.'

'Any particular reason why?' Ann didn't feel as if she was prying. She looked into his face as she asked the question, and saw a smile touch his lips.

'No particular reason. My parents are dead and my only sister is married and well taken up with her own affairs. I decided to travel around the country, staying here and there for a bit and finding out what lay in the different directions.'

'You must have some gipsy blood in you!'

'Probably.' He lapsed into silence, and Ann suppressed a shudder as a gust of cold wind tore around her. 'I saw you shiver,' he said. 'You'd better start thinking of getting out of those wet clothes or you'll be in bed with pneumonia. Let me put my raincoat around you.'

'And let your picture get wet?' Ann shook her head. 'I wouldn't hear of it, especially now you've got the composition just right.'

He smiled. 'Well you'd better start on your way again. The rain is easing, and the sooner you get into dry clothes the better.'

Ann felt another shudder run the length of her frame, and she nodded her agreement.

'Very well. I'm beginning to feel the cold. It's been nice meeting you, Doctor Lander. I hope it will turn out fine for you to finish the picture. Goodbye!'

'Goodbye, and thank you for posing for me,' he retorted.

Ann smiled and took to her heels, and she slithered on the muddy ground but kept going resolutely, and she was breathless by the time she reached the back gate to the Home. There she paused in the shelter of the wall for a moment, and when she looked back she saw him coming along behind, walking slowly, almost as carelessly as she had done, and he was holding his precious picture under his arm, covered by the raincoat. She let her features relax a little as she stared at him, taking in every detail about him. Then she shivered again and turned and went on. She didn't stop running until she reached the kitchen door of the Home, and she pushed it open and entered the building.

She had to admit there was something about Barry Lander that attracted her, and she tried to puzzle out what it was as she made her way up to her room. Perhaps it had been the way his face gentled when he smiled! Perhaps it was his blue eyes, which seemed to hold a wealth of emotion. Or it might have been his manner, so calm and pleasant. She didn't know, but she had the feeling that very soon she would find out, and she could hardly control her impatience as she considered the fact!

Chapter 3

Having bathed and changed into dry clothes, Ann felt more like herself, and she sat by the fire in her room and tried to sort out the strange feelings that had invaded her mind. Perhaps it was her homecoming that had given her elation, but she had not been as happy as this in a very long time. Even the trip home had failed to arouse her to such heights, and she puzzled over the incidents of the afternoon, thinking perhaps that the true answer lay in Barry Lander.

There was something about that man! She cut short the thought and tried to get her mind interested in something else, but she failed dismally, and there was a frown upon her lovely face as she got to her feet and went down to find her mother.

But Mrs Bowman was busy in her office with one of the patients' visitors, and Ann went on a tour of the Home, looking for familiar faces. When she saw Sister Corbin she went forward happily.

'Hello, Veronica,' she greeted.

'Ann!' Sister Corbin was tall and dark haired, a vivacious woman with a trace of youth in her face despite the fact that she was thirty-seven. 'I heard you'd arrived. I must say you're looking very well. How do you like being home?'

'I love it!' Ann's eyes glowed. 'I shan't ever go away again.'

'It doesn't seem like three years.'

'The time has gone quickly. But you were a nurse when I left. Congratulations on your promotion.'

'Thank you! I took over from Sister Mears when she left. Joy Tamworth is a Sister also. She was promoted when Sister Clarkson departed.'

'So there have been some changes.' Ann nodded. 'Doctor Hookham has gone, too, I hear.'

'You'll like Doctor Lander, who took his place,' came the swift reply. 'He's a very nice man.'

'I've already met him.' Ann did not volunteer any details.

'Oh! Well what did you think of him?'

'I thought he looked like a nice person.'

'He's engaged to marry a local girl. But I don't think you would know her.

She moved into the district after you departed.'

'I see!' There was a pang in Ann's mind that cut deeply. She hadn't expected to learn that Barry Lander was engaged. But he had been in the district over a year and it was obvious that some girl was going to snap up such a desirable man. She frowned as the thought cut across her consciousness. He was desirable! That much was obvious to her. She was disappointed, too, to learn that there was a woman in his life, and she caught her breath as she prepared to go on. 'I'd better not keep you any longer, Veronica,' she said. 'I can see you're very busy. We'll meet and have a chat later, shall we?'

'I shall look forward to it.' Sister Corbin smiled brightly and went on her way.

Ann turned and walked slowly along the corridor, her thoughts set upon Barry Lander. She couldn't help wondering at the disappointment that was spearing through her. Barry Lander was a stranger to her, and the fact that he'd spoken nicely to her this afternoon should not mean a thing. But it did mean something, she discovered, and her heart was heavy as she went on.

'Are you looking for someone, Miss?'

a voice asked her, and Ann looked up and dragged her thoughts back to her surroundings. She looked into the pretty face of a nurse, and smiled.

'No one in particular, Nurse, thank you. I'm Ann Bowman!'

'Oh, I'm sorry! I didn't know, Miss Bowman.'

'That's all right. I haven't see you before, have I?'

'I haven't been here very long. I'm Nurse Dermot.'

'How do you do?' Ann responded in friendly fashion. 'How do you like being here?'

'I think it's a wonderful place. I only wish I had come here sooner.' Nurse Dermot was tall and slim, and there was red-gold hair showing under her cap. Her frank eyes were a lovely shade of green.

'That's how I feel about the place,' Ann said with a smile. 'I'm glad to be home.'

'I've heard such a lot about you,' the girl said, nodding. 'I think your mother is very glad you've come home.'

'She is! I missed her while I was away.'

'I know the feeling,' came the steady reply. 'My mother is dead.'

'I'm sorry!' Ann stared into the girl's

friendly face with sympathy showing in her own features. She judged Nurse Dermot to be in her middle twenties. 'How do you spend your free time?'

'Well I suppose you know more about this area than I do. There isn't much to do around the village, but Wentham has more entertainment to offer.'

'You don't come from these parts?'

'London originally.'

'So does Doctor Lander.'

'Have you met the doctor?'

'Yes, I saw him this afternoon. He was painting a local scene.'

'He's a good painter! I sat for him once, and he did my portrait.'

Ann smiled. 'Perhaps he'll do one of me! But don't let me keep you now, Nurse. Sister Corbin is along the corridor, and I expect she's got her eye on you. Perhaps we can get together later and have a chat.'

'That would be nice,' the girl responded. 'I get off duty at eight this evening.'

Ann nodded, and watched the girl as she departed. There seemed to be some sort of magic in the air at the moment. Everyone was affected by it, and it made them more friendly than usual. Ann didn't think that the magic could all be in her mind. She went on and eventually found her way back to her mother's office. The door was ajar, as always during visiting hours, and Ann tapped at the centre panel, then peeped into the room.

Mrs Bowman was at her desk, sipping tea, and she set down her cup and smiled when she saw Ann.

'Come in, dear,' she said cheerfully, and got to her feet and pulled forward a chair. 'Would you like a cup of tea?'

'No thank you, but you go ahead, Mother.'

Mrs Bowman resumed her seat, and she watched Ann's face with steady brown eyes.

'What have you been doing with yourself this afternoon?'

'I went across to the farm.' Ann gave her mother a detailed account of her movements, and her dark eyes glistened as she recounted her meeting with Barry Lander.

'So you've met Barry! Do you like him?'

'I think he's very nice,' Ann replied with a smile. 'But I can't tell what he's like from a five-minute interlude with him. Didn't you say something about being worried about him when you first mentioned him?'

'I did!' Mrs Bowman nodded. 'I am worried about him. I don't suppose I ought to discuss his personal life behind his back, but I do take a motherly interest in him.'

'As you do with all the staff,' Ann said. 'I don't suppose you've changed at all in that respect, Mother!'

Mrs Bowman nodded. 'My concern helps to make for a happy, family atmosphere,' she said.

'You've certainly succeeded there. Everyone is so friendly. I spoke to Veronica Corbin just now, and then I met Nurse Dermot. I like her, but she seems a bit lonely to me.'

'It wouldn't hurt if you struck up a friendship with her. I am worried about her. She hasn't got a boyfriend, and she doesn't go out very often.'

'I'll see what I can do with her,' Ann promised. 'But why are you worried about Doctor Lander?'

There was a tap at the door at that moment, and Mrs Bowman smiled apologetically as she got to her feet.

'I'm afraid it's always like this during visiting hours, but we can talk later, Ann.'

'I'll leave you to your duties then,' Ann said, getting to her feet. She followed her mother to the door, and was surprised to see Barry Lander standing there, wearing a white coat.

'Sorry to interrupt,' he said, nodding. 'But I've just taken a look at Mrs Kirby, and I'd say her condition is deteriorating slightly. Doctor Bowman asked me to keep an eye on her this afternoon. He was afraid that she wouldn't respond to treatment.'

'Yes, we were afraid of that. I'll come with you to look at her, Doctor.' Mrs Bowman paused. 'I understand you've met Ann!'

'I had that pleasure this afternoon,' he retorted gallantly, smiling at Ann, and she felt her pulses race for a moment. Then she told herself that he was engaged to someone, and her interest waned quickly. She took a deep breath as she smiled in reply, and his blue eyes narrowed for a moment as he studied her face. 'I managed to get her into the picture I'm painting.'

'I'm sure I've ruined that for you,' Ann retorted. She was trying to imagine the kind of girl who would interest him.

'You could only make it that much better,' he replied lightly.

Ann followed them from the room, and she paused and watched her mother walking along the corridor beside his tall figure. A sudden longing touched her heart and she sighed deeply. She hadn't known what to expect upon her arrival home. She feared that she would look back with regret upon the sunny days she'd turned her back upon. But already she was pleased at being home, and there seemed to be a sharp eagerness somewhere inside that prompted her to all kinds of wild and extravagant thoughts.

She went back to her room and sat down to clear her mind. She was attracted to Barry Lander! That thought stood out above all others. But she would have to fight that attraction from the very beginning because if she let it take root then she would be heading for disaster. She mused upon the past, and tried to find any kind of emotion that had gripped her when she'd been in love with Gerry. But her thoughts were clear and unruffled, and she couldn't find the slightest pang of regret or anything else for the past and the broken dreams which it contained.

Shortly after tea her father returned, and Ann was delighted to see him. He swept her into his arms and kissed her hard, then held her at arm's length and studied her critically. He was tall and heavily built, and looking more like his brother Charles than Ann remembered. She commented upon the fact.

'I went across to the farm and saw Uncle Charles this afternoon,' she said. 'You two must be twins, Father. I've never seen two brothers look more alike and not be twins.'

'What did Charles have to say to you?'

'He was very pleased to see me!'

'And so am I.' He kissed her again. 'Your mother and I have missed you dreadfully, Ann. You were the only thing we lacked in this world, but now you've come back to us.' He paused and studied her for a moment. 'You're not home just for a short holiday, are you?' he demanded. 'You're really home for good?'

'Completely! I'll never go away again.' She hugged him, her emotions aroused, and she gave a tender smile as she moved breathless away from him. 'This place has improved in the last three years,' she commented. 'You're doing very well, aren't you, Father?'

'Very well indeed! I'm satisfied.'

'Then you must be doing extremely well for you to admit that,' she retorted. 'But you've devoted yourself to this project and you deserve success.'

'What are your plans now you're home, or is it too early to ask?' He took her hand and led her to the settee, where they sat close together. Ann had always been very close to her parents, and she loved them intensely. They had always been very attentive and loving to her, and it showed now in their manner towards one another.

'I expect I'll work here with you, if there's a position for me,' she said.

'Of course there's a place for you. It's always been my greatest ambition to have you working here with us.'

'Then you ambition is about to be realized.' Ann smiled. 'I think I'll have two weeks holiday before getting into harness again. I want to have a look around and see the old friends I've missed over the past three years.'

'What about Gerry?' he demanded.

'That's completely over and done with,' she replied.

'I'm sorry. But it's better that you found out it was a mistake before you married him, Ann.'

'That is a blessing,' she agreed. 'I didn't have a bad time over it, or anything like that. He just didn't love me, and I think I must have fallen out of love with him somewhere along the line without realizing it.'

'Welcome home, anyway.' His dark eyes were filled with sharp pleasure. 'At last we're a complete family again.' He sighed as he glanced at his watch. 'Not that we ever have much chance of a normal family life, but that can't be helped in this business. I must ask you to excuse me now, Ann, because there are some patients I must look at. But I had to come up here and see you first.'

Ann nodded her understanding, and walked with him to the door. He departed with a smiling backward glance, and she felt her happiness bubbling up inside as she watched his tall figure. A sigh gusted through her and she felt many undefinable impressions lurking in her brain.

Not many minutes later her mother came into the sitting room, and Mrs Bowman had changed out of her uniform.

She smiled a little tiredly at Ann, and came and sat down at her daughter's side.

'I've just seen your father,' she said. 'He's happy now you're home. I've been wondering what was wrong with him for months, and now I know. He's been missing you badly, Ann.'

'Has he?' Ann's face softened as she looked into her mother's brown eyes. 'I missed both of you, but I'm home now and we can put the past behind us. Father was saying I can have a job here with you if I want it.'

'You wouldn't think of going anywhere else to work, would you?'

'No. You can put me on the strength as soon as you like.'

'You're taking a holiday first, surely!'

'Yes. I thought two weeks would suffice.'

'You'll need a car to get around in,' Mrs Bowman said. 'I rarely use mine now, and I can borrow Father's if I ever need to go into town when he's on duty. So you can take over my car if you wish to.'

'What sort of a car is it?' Ann demanded.

'It's a Fiat 124! I find it a very comfortable car, and it's white. That's your favourite colour in a car, if I remember.'

Ann nodded. 'Thank you, Mother. But I expect my driving licence has expired. I'll have to get it renewed before I start driving again. But I'll look forward to getting on road, especially being able to drive myself alone.'

'You always did like getting away by yourself,' Mrs Bowman said musingly. 'But you haven't come to any harm, have you?'

'None at all. Are you off duty now?'

'Yes, thank Heaven! I begin to feel my age now, Ann.'

'Nonsense! You're not an old woman yet, not by a long chalk.'

'I'm getting older, and the end of each day tells me so.'

Ann nodded, studying her mother's clear face intently. There were crowsfeet at the corners of her mother's eyes, but no grey hairs showed yet, and Ann watched her mother critically for a few moments.

'Would you like to go into town this evening?' Mrs Bowman asked.

'I'm not going to drag you out after you've finished for the day, and I can't drive until I've got another licence.' Ann shook her head. 'I don't think I shall bother, although it would be nice to take a look around again. Three years does take quite a chunk out of one's life.'

'Doctor Lander—Barry, goes into town quite often to see his fiancee, and I asked him if he'd mind dropping you in town if you want to go, to save me turning out. He agreed, and if you'll be ready at six-thirty he'll take you in.'

'That's kind of him!' Ann felt her heart start pounding at the thought. She glanced at her watch. 'It doesn't give me much time to get ready, but how shall I get back later?'

'Barry will bring you back. He's never very late coming in.'

'Then I'd better start getting ready.' Ann got to her feet and started for the door. 'If he comes enquiring for me tell him I won't keep him long.'

Mrs Bowman nodded and smiled as Ann left the room.

It didn't take Ann long to get ready, and she was back in the sitting room just before six-thirty, feeling a little bit surprised when she found Barry Lander sitting with her mother and chatting easily and animatedly. He was obviously waiting for her, and Ann felt her cheeks burn as she paused in the doorway and looked at him.

'It's kind of you to give me a lift, Doctor,' she said quickly. 'I don't have a current driving licence at the moment.'

'That's all right. I'm going into town anyway, and I'll have an empty car.' He glanced at his watch, and for a moment his pale blue eyes showed approval. 'And you're right on time. That shows good training.'

'I'd hate to keep you waiting,' she retorted.

He smiled as he took his leave of Mrs Bowman, and Ann crossed the room to her mother's side and kissed her cheek.

'I'll bring you back, of course,' Barry said from the doorway. 'That's if you're not too late. I'm an early bird myself.'

'I'm only going to look up some old friends,' Ann said, smiling.

Mrs Bowman walked to the door with her, and Ann kissed her mother once more before they parted.

'Take care of yourself,' Mrs Bowman called, and Ann nodded and waved an acknowledging hand as she walked along the corridor at Barry's side.

There was a strange sensation in Ann's breast as she accompanied Barry from the Home. His car was outside the front door, and he took her arm as she descended the steps, which were wet and slippery. When she was safely ensconced in the car he slammed the door upon her and went around to his seat. The evening was damp and cold, and despite the warm clothing she was wearing, Ann felt the cold. But she watched Barry's face as he settled himself in his seat and then started the car.

They didn't have much to say to one another on the five miles trip to town. Ann was keenly aware of his presence, and she found her thoughts disconcerting as she tried to get her mind to concentrate on anything but the man at her side. Her emotions were upset by her homecoming, she thought swiftly. That had to be the cause of this unrest she was feeling. She was pleased and happy at being home, and this was the way her mind had of showing her feelings.

'You'll have a lot of friends to look up, no doubt,' he said at length.

'There used to be quite a number before I went away, but three years can make a lot of difference in things like that. I expect some of our old gang have gone away.'

The lights of Wentham showed yellowly

in the distance, and Ann caught her breath as she tried to stop her elation rising too high.

'Where would you like me to set you down?'

'Oh!' she paused to think. 'It doesn't really matter. Anywhere in the town centre will do. I suppose I ought to have made some telephone calls before coming out in case I can't raise anyone. I didn't think.'

'You're probably too excited,' he said slowly.

When they reached the town centre Barry stopped the car near the small market place, and Ann made haste to alight.

'Just a moment,' he said quickly. 'You'll want a ride back later, won't you?'

'Oh yes! I'd be in a fine pickle if I rushed of without making arrangements. What time will you go back to the Home?'

'What time will you be ready to?' he countered.

'It's your car and you're doing me a good turn,' she retorted. 'I shall await your convenience.'

'It doesn't matter to me!' He spoke lightly, but she detected a trace of tension in his tones.

'Say ten-thirty then!'

'At this very spot.' He smiled at her. 'I'll be waiting for you.'

'Thank you, Doctor.'

'Not Doctor!' His tones were curt. 'My name is Barry.'

'All right, Barry, and thanks a lot.'

'It's my pleasure.' He smiled gravely. 'Have a nice time.'

'I will. I've waited three years for this moment.' She stepped back and slammed the door, and he drove away quickly.

Ann slowly became aware that it was raining again, and she stood watching Barry's car vanish into the night. When the vehicle had passed from sight she sighed heavily for no apparent reason and looked around, breathing deeply as she did so. What was she going to do? She'd jumped at the chance of getting a ride in Barry's car, and yet she'd made no plans for her evening. She moved to a shop doorway to shelter from the rain and tried to think of her old circle of friends.

The first person who came to mind was Petra Grahame, and Ann smiled as she considered her friend. Petra had promised to write regularly after Ann went away, but after a letter or two had arrived a silence followed. Ann sighed again, and now she was beginning to feel a bit despondent. She didn't appear to have a friend in the world. Gerry was gone into the past! She felt a twinge of pain at the thought and tried to dismiss it summarily. Self pity wouldn't help, she told herself firmly. She had come home to make a new life for herself, and that was what she intended doing.

Rain splashed into her face as she walked along the darkened street, and she was relieved when she reached a telephone box. She found Petra's number in the directory and called, a smile of anticipation on her face as she waited. When the receiver was lifted at the other end, Petra's voice sounded in her ear, and Ann recognized the voice instantly.

'Hello, Petra,' she said cheerfully. 'It's a long time since I heard your voice. How are you these days?'

'Who's that?' came the swift reply.

'Surely you can recognize my tones!' Ann was smiling broadly.

'It isn't Ann Bowman!'

'It is! How are you, Petra?'

'Just fine! How are you, Ann? How long have you been home? You're not calling from across the world, are you?'

'No. I'm here in town. What are you doing this evening? I thought I'd look up a few old friends. I came home earlier today.'

'Well you know where I live. Come round. I'm going to a party this evening, but you can come along, too. It's given by Hugh Leighton. You remember Hugh!'

'Yes, I remember him very well. Weren't you going to marry him at one time?'

'I was until he fell in love with you. But you went off with your Gerry, and when Hugh tried to come back to me afterwards I refused to have anything to do with him. We're still very good friends though, and he's often asked after you, as a matter of fact.'

'We seemed to lose contact for some reason or other,' Ann said with a chuckle. 'But never mind. I'm home again and I'm staying.'

'What about Gerry?'

'That's finished.'

'I'm sorry, Ann! You were very fond of him, weren't you?'

'I was at the beginning, but it wore off, so there are no regrets and no heartbreak. Look, I'll walk round to your place right away. You can expect me in a couple of minutes.'

'I'll be here,' Petra promised, and the line went dead.

Ann sighed a little as she walked to the street where Petra's flat was situated. Here she was about to pick up the severed threads of her life, threads she had imagined were severed for good. But she was back where she belonged, and she intended that there would be no mistakes in future. She wouldn't put a foot wrong anywhere.

Yet as she spoke she thought unconsciously of Barry Lander, and she sighed as she faced the fact that she liked him against all her instincts. She didn't like the knowledge that he was engaged to be married! That was something she hadn't counted on that afternoon when she'd met him at the brook. He'd seemed wistful in some intangible way, and she had begun to think that perhaps he'd had an unhappy romance. But that couldn't be the reason for his background mood, his atmosphere that no amount of smiling would banish. There had to be something else, and it puzzled her to think about it.

However this evening she meant to enjoy

herself, for it would be the first time in months. Tonight she was going to plunge into the swim again, and she hoped she'd like the temperature of the water!

Chapter Four

Petra Grahame hadn't seemed to have changed a bit when Ann saw her. The girl opened the door of her flat and Ann felt that it had been only yesterday when they'd last met.

'Ann! You look wonderful! Look at that lovely tan! I spent three weeks in August in the South of France and I didn't get anything near to your colour. The tropics certainly agree with you. What on earth did you come home for? There's nothing but Autumn and Winter waiting for you here.'

'It's a relief to get back, and I thoroughly enjoyed the shower I was caught in this afternoon,' Ann replied. 'You can have too much of a good thing, you know.'

'I won't believe that!' Petra took Ann's arm and led her into the flat. 'Listen, I rang Hugh and told him you were back, and he said he'd break my neck if I didn't take you along to his party tonight.'

'I'd love to go with you, of course,'

Ann replied. 'But I'm hardly dressed for party-going.'

'Don't worry about that. There'll be several of the old gang there, and they'll all be very happy to see you again. You were always being talked about.'

'I can well believe that,' Ann said with a laugh. 'But tell me what's been happening to you in the past three years. You're obviously not married yet! Are you going steady, Petra?'

'No!' The girl sighed heavily. 'I haven't seen anyone yet I could go into raptures over. But it doesn't matter about me. I want to hear about you! All that sunshine and a beautiful island. Life must have been like one long holiday.'

'I think I had something like that in mind when I left this country,' Ann said, shaking her head. 'But I soon discovered that it wasn't like that at all. Life goes on much the same there as it does anywhere, and people have to work. The glorious conditions and scenery made work seem all the more irksome sometimes.'

'I can't believe it! I'd take your place over there tomorrow if I could.' Petra smiled as she led the way into her small sitting room. 'We've got half an hour before we have to leave, so sit down and bring me up to date with what's been happening to you.'

Ann nodded, and she talked incessantly for the allotted thirty minutes. Then she began to ask questions, and Petra shook her head carelessly.

'Nothing ever happens to any of us, you know,' she said. 'We live in very small circles and do much the same thing day after day and week after week. Rosemary Manning got married last year. You knew Giles Harper, didn't you? Of course you did! He's an accountant, and they're doing quite well. Let me think! Who else has got married whom you might know? Geraldine Spooner! She married a police inspector and moved away from the area. I heard some months ago that she's got a baby boy. Some of the gang have moved away. Billy Anders comes back regularly to see us. He's in London doing something in advertising. So you see you're not the only one who has been caught up by life and taken away. And you've come back to us! I can't still quite believe it, Ann. I didn't think we'd ever meet again this side of Heaven.'

Ann looked into her friend's grey eyes

and smiled. Petra was an ash-blonde with a peach complexion. She was tall and willowy, almost too beautiful to be true, and Ann couldn't understand why the girl hadn't found romance in a big way.

'What are you doing for a living these days, Petra?' she asked.

'You passed the shop down below. The boutique is mine. I run it with Sara Bland! I don't think you know Sara. She isn't one of the old gang.' Petra ran on while she got up to put the finishing touches to her make up. Then she glanced at her watch. 'I think we can leave now. We want to get to Hugh's fairly early because he'll want to talk to you before the party gets under way.'

'I shall be leaving early,' Ann said as they left the flat. 'I have arranged a lift back to the Home.'

'Who's taking you?'

'One of the doctors at the Home.'

'There's only one other beside your father, isn't there?'

'Yes. Doctor Lander.'

'What's he like? Is he young and good looking?'

'Yes, I do believe he is! But he's engaged to be married, I think!'

'That's a pity. I've always fancied myself as the wife of a doctor. Who's he engaged to?'

'I don't know.' Ann smiled as they went along the street, and they caught a bus to the other side of town.

Petra chattered away nineteen to the dozen, informing Ann of everything of importance that had happened in the three years she'd been away, and she talked about a lot of people Ann had never heard of. But it was all the same to Petra, and Ann smiled to herself as she realized that the girl hadn't changed a bit. But there was no spite in Petra Grahame! Ann liked the girl and she was glad Petra was not married so they could start going around together again.

Hugh Leighton lived in an exclusive block of flats in a smart area, and Ann took a deep breath as she waited at the door of his flat while Petra rang the bell. She was recalling Hugh, and she remembered that he had been very ardent about her before Gerry came upon the scene. Well she liked Hugh, but there was a picture of Barry Lander's face in her mind as the door opened and Hugh appeared before them.

Hugh Leighton was medium-sized, and smaller than Ann remembered him. He had beetling brows and dark, expressive eyes, and seemed almost as wide as he was tall. He had put on a lot of weight, Ann thought as she looked into his face, and he extended a fleshy hand towards her and smiled.

'Ann! Ann Bowman! You're a sight for sore eyes.' He paused and looked at Petra. 'Go on in and make yourself at home, Petra,' he commanded. 'I want to have a few words with Ann before I turn the rest of the party loose on her.'

'Are they all here?' Petra demanded, winking at Ann. She went into the flat and Ann could hear the sounds of music emanating from within.

'I wish we could find somewhere quiet to talk, but I'm afraid that's impossible this evening,' Hugh said. He looked into Ann's face. 'You've got a lovely tan. All that Caribbean sunshine, I suppose. You haven't changed a bit though. You're even lovelier than ever! I can hardly get over the shock of learning that you're back. I'd really given you up for lost, Ann.'

'Well I'm back for good, and as large as life,' she retorted. 'I must say you're looking very well, Hugh.'

'I can't grumble. I'm going all right in business. Did you know my father had died? There's a great deal of money to be made in printing these days, and the business is all mine now.'

'I'm sorry about your father, but he was never a robust man, was he?'

'No! He would have done a lot more in life if he'd had full health. But I'm making up for what he couldn't do.'

'You must be doing very well then!' Ann was remembering that he always was something of a braggart, but he was well meaning and hard working, so he deserved all he got. 'But haven't you had time to find a wife? All work and no play, you know.'

'I could have made the time, but when you went away there wasn't anyone else for me. I couldn't make do with second best.' His face was serious, and Ann forced a smile.

'Now you're flattering me!' she accused.

'No!' He was deadly serious. 'You know you always meant a great deal to me, Ann.'

She was relieved when footsteps sounded on the stairs, and a moment later someone called Hugh's name. She turned, but she didn't recognize the couple coming towards them. But Hugh laughed lightly.

'Teddy! Ilona! I'm glad you two could make it. I'm sure you've heard me talking about Ann Bowman many times in the past, and sometimes I've bored you with singing her praises. Well now you can meet her in person, and tell me if I did her full justice. This is Ann. Ann, I want you to meet Teddy and Ilona Barrett. Teddy is a business associate now.'

They all shook hands, and Ann was relieved that Hugh had been interrupted. But she warned herself that he would make another attempt to monopolize her, and she guessed that he intended trying to take up where he had left off three years before. He's always had a soft spot for her, and even when she had told him she was engaged to marry Gerry he had tried to get her to leave her fiancée. He was a most persistent man, but he had never been more than a friend to Ann.

There were a number of old friends at the party, and Ann was very pleased to see them again. She spent a good deal of her time relating some of her experiences abroad, and describing the weather and scenery. Hugh kept her supplied with drinks, and she put them aside whenever possible, or passed them to Petra, who seemed to drink continuously without adverse effect.

All too soon it was time to go, and Ann sought out Petra and explained.

'All right, Ann. I'm sorry to see you leaving so soon, but give me a ring in a day or so and we'll make arrangements to get together. You'd better say goodbye to Hugh, if you can find him.'

Ann nodded and smiled and looked around the large room. Hugh was not to be seen, so she went along to the kitchen, and there she found the host, deeply engaged in conversation with a beautiful blonde girl.

'Ann, is something wrong?' Hugh demanded instantly, coming to her side.

'Nothing, thank you, Hugh! But it's time I departed.'

'You can't leave yet!' He glanced at his watch. 'The party has hardly started.'

'I'm sorry but I had no idea I was coming here when I left home earlier, and I did make other arrangements.'

'Then telephone and cancel them.'

'I can't do that.'

'If it's a case of getting home later then I can drive you.'

'I shouldn't think you'll be in a fit state to drive later, will you, Hugh?' she countered.

He sighed heavily and shook his head. 'Perhaps you're right. But I'm not going to lose sight of you now you're home. I shall want to see you again. What about tomorrow evening?'

'I don't know. My parents are making some arrangements for a family get-together, I'm sure, so I'd better not add complications by making promises.'

'Well you have my telephone number at the office, don't you?' He was beginning to accept that she intended slipping away immediately.

'I can get it out of the book. Thank you for a nice evening, Hugh.'

'I'll see you to the door.' He took her arm and squeezed it as he led her along the hall. 'Goodnight, Ann, and I'm so happy you've come home.'

'Goodnight, Hugh. It's been very pleasant seeing you again.'

She slipped out through the half open door and departed hurriedly, glancing at her watch and seeing that the time was

84

almost ten-thirty. She didn't want to keep Barry waiting. A sigh escaped her as she hurried out to the street, and she was relieved when a bus arrived almost as soon as she reached the nearest stop. Her mind churned over the events of the evening, and she felt elated, very pleased that she had come home. But she was afraid that Hugh might start putting pressure on her now he'd seen her again. She smiled slowly as she thought of the way he had always seemed to want her.

When she alighted at the town centre she saw Barry's car parked at the spot he'd said he'd be, and she sighed with relief and hurried across the road. She peeped through the window at Barry, who was seated behind the wheel, and he turned his head and smiled, his teeth glinting in the light reflected from a nearby street lamp. He opened the door for her and she slipped into the vehicle at his side.

'Sorry I'm a bit late,' she said instantly.

'That's all right. I'm in no hurry.' He started the car and a blast of hot air struck her legs, making her shiver. 'Have you enjoyed yourself this evening?'

'Yes thank you. Very much. I've met a lot of old friends.'

'That's good. One should enjoy oneself when one is young.'

'Oh!' She glanced at him. 'That makes you sound as if you're well over one hundred years old!'

'Does it?' He smiled, but there was no joy in his features, and Ann watched him while he drove to the outskirts of town. The street lighting showed his face plainly, and she thought he looked rather miserable for a man who had just spent the evening with his fiancée.

'Haven't you had a nice time?' she demanded.

'Me?' He glanced at her. They were coming to the end of the street lights, and blackness awaited them beyond the town limits. 'I didn't come out tonight to enjoy myself.'

'I'm sorry. Perhaps I was labouring under a delusion.'

'You mean you heard that I'm engaged to be married and you naturally assumed that I was coming into town to spend the evening with my fiancée.'

'Well, yes!'

'My fiancée doesn't live in town. When your mother asked me if I'd drive you into town I agreed. I wasn't going out

86

this evening. But then I thought it would be nice to get away from the Home for a spell.'

'What did you do with yourself all night then?' Ann demanded. She frowned as she stared at his profile.

'I like driving, especially at night and during this kind of weather. I went for a drive and returned in time to collect you.'

'That makes me feel awful,' she said instantly. 'Why on earth did you do it?'

'Because I knew your mother would be too tired to turn out to drive you, and your father is on duty. I guessed your driving licence would be out of date and you were so kind to me this afternoon that I couldn't spoil your evening by thinking of myself.'

'You're a strange man, Doctor!'

'Barry,' he retorted.

'Barry. Where on earth did you go this evening? You had four hours to kill. Surely you didn't drive around all the time?'

'I did. I told you, I like driving.' He chuckled, but his tone was harsh.

'Aren't you happy at the Home? 'Ann asked.

'Why do you ask that?'

'Because you don't sound like a happy

87

man. Yet when I met you this afternoon I thought you were an exceedingly happy man.'

'Did you?' His chuckle this time was softer, and the sound of it sent a thrill through Ann. 'That was probably because I was doing what I love best.'

'Painting!' She frowned. 'Aren't you happy as a doctor?'

'Oh yes! Medicine is my whole life.' He glanced at her, and the car seemed to be rushing through a brightly lit tunnel. Darkness hemmed them in upon all sides, and Ann could vaguely glimpse the darker shadows of trees overhanging the road. 'But because one loves medicine it doesn't follow that all other pursuits are abandoned.'

'Of course not!' She agreed instantly. 'I love nursing. I can't wait to get back into uniform and on duty.'

'Really?'

'Yes! Don't you believe me?'

'Certainly. But there's no need for you to nurse, is there?'

'Why ever not? Just because my parents own the nursing home?' Ann shook her head sharply. 'Don't get the wrong impression of me, Barry. When I go on duty at the Home I shall work as hard and as long as anyone.'

'You will. I can see you're that kind of a girl! Forgive me! Perhaps I was thinking out aloud. I ought not to have said that.'

Ann lapsed into silence, and there was a frown on her face as she considered his words. He sounded thoroughly out of humour now, and she wondered what had upset him. But she couldn't get over the fact that he had turned out this evening just to transport her to and from town. It was a magnificent gesture, and her heart was thrilled by the knowledge. But she was certain all was not well in his world, and when she pictured his face as she had seen him that afternoon by the brook she felt sad.

Presently they came in sight of Clover House, and Ann was sorry they had arrived. She would have enjoyed her evening all the more if she'd been in his company during the length of it. A sigh gusted through her and she firmed her lips as he brought the car to a halt before the front entrance.

'Perhaps we'd better go in the side door,' she suggested. 'I wouldn't want to disturb the patients. It is getting late.'

He nodded and drove around the

concrete path. There was a lamp burning over the side door, and it threw a dim circle of light over the doorway, but created dense shadows beyond the circle. Ann held her breath for a moment, then released it in a long sigh. The car stopped and he turned to look at her.

'Thank you,' she said softly. 'It was very kind of you to do what you did tonight.'

'You can repay me if you wish.' His voice was pitched low.

'Certainly!'

'Don't tell your mother about it.'

'Oh!' Ann stared at him with a frown on her face. 'All right. You know your own business best. I won't mention it to Mother.' She paused for a moment longer, looking into his face. But his eyes were invisible, lost in thick shadows, his face showing no expression whatever. 'Thank you again. But I do feel awfully guilty about your evening.'

'I had nothing else to do, Ann!' He smiled. 'Now you'd better go in. It is getting late and you've had a lot of excitement.'

'Goodnight!' She dragged her eyes from his face and alighted from the car, hurrying across to the door and entering the building

90

without so much as a backward glance, but she was thinking of him as she went along to the private wing and looked into the sitting room to see if her parents were still up.

Mrs Bowman was seated in an easy chair, reading a nursing magazine, which she put aside when Ann entered the room. Ann frowned at the sight of her mother.

'You haven't waited up for me to get in, have you, Mother?' she demanded. 'You look exhausted. You should have gone to bed an hour ago.'

'I am feeling tired, but that's a natural occurrence every night. I don't give in to it.' Mrs Bowman smiled. 'I just wanted to see you come in. It's been such a long time since I waited up for you.'

'Poor Mother! I didn't realize when I went away that you would miss me. I was all right. It was all happening to me, but you had to stay behind and do the suffering.'

'It's a mother's lot, and I'm not alone in that. It happens to all parents at some time or other. Children grow up and have to make their own way through life. A parent's duty is to see the child reaches maturity with all the essential lessons learned. I think your father and I did a good job on you.'

'I know you did!' Ann crossed to her mother's side and sat down. She kissed her mother's cheek. 'I'm eternally grateful for the way I was brought up. I had all the chances. I never lacked anything. You gave me all the love and affection I needed, and I seem to have done nothing for you in return. I went off and left you for three years, causing you heartache. What a way to repay what you did for me!'

'Nonsense.' Mrs Bowman stroked Ann's tanned cheek. There was a smile on her lips and a soft light in her dark eyes. 'You've given me the opportunity of seeing myself again as I was when in my youth. A mother can ask for no more than that, Ann. There is a higher purpose in life than the reasons we put forward as humans. We make our lives as best we can, and usually for our own comfort and to our own satisfaction. But we know very little of the wider reasons for our being, and we can only do what we can and hope it is our best and for the general good.'

'You're getting very serious now,' Ann said lightly.

'Sorry! It must be because I'm tired. But

now you're in I'll go to bed. Goodnight, my sweet! It's so nice to have you home again. Tomorrow you can tell me all about your evening. I'm sure you're quite happy now.'

'I am, Mother!' Ann rose as her mother got to her feet. 'I've never been happier. I only wish I had come back home long ago, or that I hadn't even gone away.'

'You've been and you saw. The time you spent must have been repaid by the experience.' Mrs Bowman kissed Ann's cheek and departed, and Ann went into the kitchen to get herself a drink.

She was thoughtful as she prepared to go to bed. It had been a momentous day, and she let her agile mind roam back over everything that had happened. Life had gone on here in England while she had been away, and now she was back home life was going on just the same out there where she had left Gerry. She had a sudden mental picture of time and space that was so vast as to stagger her, and she sighed as she shook her head tiredly and made her way to her room.

Tomorrow could take care of itself. Right now she was tired and ready for bed, and even the thoughts of Barry Lander now failed to raise any flicker of emotion inside her. But he was on her mind as she lay relaxed and waiting for slumber to overtake her. She even dreamed about him during the long night, although next morning she could not recall the fact clearly. But time was waiting to unfold the next phase of her life, and she could only wait and hope and wonder what it might be. She could not cross the unscalable barrier of time to peer into the future. All she could do was pray that she would not make any mistakes. If she avoided the pitfalls then she could find herself with much to applaud. It was as simple as that.

Chapter Five

Next morning Ann set out to really explore her home surroundings, and she recalled many happy memories as she wandered about the grounds of Clover House and also the surrounding fields. But the past was tied up with Gerry, and she found difficulty in separating the two in her mind. However it was a happy time, and when she returned to the Home for lunch she was in high spirits.

Now that she was home she could start planning her future. It was great to be able to look beyond a certain point and say that it would be nice to follow a particular course. Before she had come home she had faced the barrier of the journey itself and the transitional period between the two worlds. She hadn't been able to look beyond this particular day, and now it had arrived she found all boundaries well and truly removed.

She had lunch with her parents, and was about to depart for an afternoon when her mother called her to the telephone.

'It's Hugh Leighton,' Mrs Bowman said, holding out the receiver with a steady hand. 'You haven't had time to tell me about your evening last night, but I presume Hugh was one of the old friends you met again.'

'He was!' Ann smiled as she took the instrument, and Mrs Bowman departed into the sitting room. But the smile faded a little as Ann gave her name.

'Ann!' Leighton sounded very pleased. 'It's nice to hear your voice again. I was thinking this morning that perhaps I'd dreamed about you last night, so I had to call just to set my mind at rest. It's so wonderful to hear your voice. When am I going to see you again? May I call out at the Home this evening and see you?'

'Well I still don't know if I'll be otherwise engaged,' Ann replied. 'I haven't had the chance to talk things over with my mother.'

'I'll hang on while you ask her,' he prompted, and chuckled. 'I promise you I won't let the grass grow under my feet.'

Ann thought of Barry Lander while she considered, and for some unknown reason she didn't want to get involved with Hugh. There was no chance for her with Barry!

The thought put colour into her cheeks. Did she want a chance with him? Only a few days ago she had bid Gerry a calm goodbye, and she'd been telling herself ever since that she wanted no more romantic entanglements. Now, on her second day at home, she was wondering speculatively about a stranger.

'Are you still there, Ann?' Hugh demanded.

'Yes. Sorry, Hugh. Look, I don't want to raise your hopes, but I do know we're having a family get together and very probably tonight. Will you let me be home a few days before trying to monopolize my time.'

'All right!' He was most reluctant to accept her word, but he couldn't disagree. 'I'll call you again in a few days. But I can hardly wait to see you again. Goodbye now, and expect to hear from me some time on Friday.' He paused. 'That's giving you two days to find your feet. Then I'm going to expect to share some of your time.'

'Goodbye then,' she said, and waited until the line went dead before hanging up.

Going into the sitting room, Ann faced her mother.

'You look as if you've got to make an important decision,' Mrs Bowman commented.

'I don't know about that!' Ann shook her head.

'Hugh was always sweet on you, wasn't he? I suppose he plans to get in first this time.'

'I've never liked Hugh enough to want him to get romantic.' Ann said slowly, thoughtfully. 'Oh, I like him well enough, but I don't think I could ever fall in love with him.'

'Then I suggest you let him know that before he starts getting ideas.'

'Perhaps you're right. He's going to call me on Friday. I'll see him and let him know what the situation is, but I'm afraid he'll still be as hard to convince of something he doesn't want to know about as he was before I went away. Have you called Uncle Charles yet, Mother?'

'I'm going to telephone right now,' Mrs Bowman replied, and she went into the hall. Ann followed, and stood by while her mother rang Clover Farm. 'Hello, Charles, this is Eileen. When are you coming over for the evening? Yes, we're both off duty this evening, and Ann will be here. Fine. We'll expect you about seven-thirty. Goodbye now.'

'Well that was short and sweet,' Ann said with a smile as her mother replaced the receiver.

'I know he's so busy during the day,' Mrs Bowman replied. 'He has told me off before about wasting his time when he's got other things to do.'

'So he's coming across this evening, and I expect Paul will bring his fiancée along. Have you ever met her, Mother?'

'Yes, I have, and she's an extremely pleasant girl. If Paul lets her down then he'll be the biggest fool ever.'

'I think he's settled down now,' Ann said confidently. 'When I saw him yesterday I was amazed at the sight of him. He looks as if butter wouldn't melt in his mouth now.'

'You'll be here this evening then?' Mrs Bowman asked.

'Yes. I haven't made any arrangements.'

'Then I'd better go back on duty. I can't sit around all afternoon!'

'I think I'll take just the rest of this week and start working next Monday,' Ann retorted. 'My days will start dragging if I'm wandering around too much.'

'Just as you like. Father and I were talking about you last night. Sister Tamworth is leaving us next Easter to get married. We can see how you work between now and then, and if you've got the necessary experience you can take Sister Tamworth's place.'

'That will be nice!' Ann smiled. 'There's nothing like having your parents as your superiors.'

'You know you wouldn't get the position unless you qualified for it, don't you?'

'Of course, Mother! I wouldn't want it any other way.' Ann nodded.

'I shall be off duty at five. What are you going to do with yourself until then?'

'I thought I might go into town and see about getting my driving licence renewed.'

'But you can't drive yourself in without it. I wonder if Barry is going into town this afternoon.'

'Mother, I can't put upon him like that. He was very kind to take me in last night.' Ann frowned as she recalled the sad mood Barry had appeared to be in when he'd brought her home. He'd wasted the entire evening just waiting around for her.

'He's very nice, and he won't mind what he does for you.'

100

'Twice yesterday you began to tell me why you were worried about him, Mother, but each time you were interrupted. Has he got any troubles?'

'I don't know for certain, but I wouldn't be surprised. He hasn't seemed very happy since he became engaged. Perhaps he's not ready for marriage yet. He did say he'd have to leave here if he married. His future wife wouldn't want to stay in these parts.'

'She's not a local girl anyway, is she?'

'I don't think so. I haven't asked any questions, but from what Barry has said at odd times I don't think she likes the country.' Mrs Bowman shook her head thoughtfully. 'I believe she's using Barry to get away from here. She moved here with her parents last year, it seems, and she doesn't like it enough to want to stay. Barry said he didn't care where he lived, so she's gradually got him into a position where he's cornered. I feel so sorry for him. He's such a nice person.'

Ann nodded slowly. She had come to a similar decision about him.

'I'll go and ask him what he's doing this afternoon. You need to get your driving licence renewed and then you won't have

101

to rely on anyone for a lift.'

'Please don't bother him, Mother,' Ann said.

'It won't be any bother. I like to keep him busy when he's off duty and he isn't seeing his fiancée. If he stays around here he mopes a lot. At least, I think he's moping, although he'll never admit to it.'

'Poor Barry! If you treat him like this all the time then his life must be a misery. No wonder he mopes, Mother!'

Mrs Bowman smiled and departed, and Ann frowned as she considered. There were some strange impressions in the back of her mind and she didn't know exactly what they related to.

Some minutes later there was a tap at the door, and Ann opened it quickly, half expecting it to be Barry, and her heart seemed to miss a beat when she found herself looking into his face.

'Hello,' she said quickly.

'Hello.' He smiled, and his blue eyes shone momentarily. 'I was just talking to your mother.'

'Won't you come in?' Ann invited. 'You're off duty, aren't you?'

'Yes. I go back on duty at five today. I'll run you into town if you wish.'

'It's very kind of you, but I can't impose upon you, especially after last evening. It isn't fair on you! Mother thinks she's doing you a good turn by keeping you occupied, but she doesn't know the half of it, does she?'

'You're right.' He smiled as he entered the room, and Ann closed the door at his back. 'She only knows what I want her to know. But if your licence needs renewing then you'd better get it done. You never know when you may want to go dashing off in a car.'

'Well if you're sure it will be no inconvenience,' she said slowly.

'None at all. In fact it will help me take my mind off things. It's too dull for me to go painting this afternoon. I was toying with the idea of going into town, anyway.'

'All right. Are you ready to leave now?'

'As soon as you are!' He smiled, then glanced at his watch, and Ann felt a tremor worming its way through her. 'I have to be back here about four to get ready for duty.'

'I have only to put on my coat, and find the old licence,' she explained. 'Would you care to sit down while I get ready?'

'I'll go and get the car out. Perhaps you'll come out to the front. I expect you'll be ready by the time I have the car out of the garage.'

'All right.' She smiled at him, but she wasn't feeling as cool and collected as she appeared. Her pulses were racing, and she was looking forward to sitting by his side in the car.

She let him out and then hurried to get ready. She found her driving licence in an old wallet which she used for storing old papers and letters, and checked that she had some cash with her. Then she hurried down to the front entrance, thrilled by the knowledge that she was going off in his company.

Ann found Barry waiting for her, seated in the car in front of the steps, and she caught her breath as she joined him. The smile he gave her as she slid into the car at his side set her nerves fluttering, and she moistened her lips as she closed the door and locked it.

'That didn't take long,' he commented, smiling as he glanced at her, and Ann told herself that he looked happier today. 'Have you got your licence with you?'

'Yes. I had no trouble finding it. It's

104

completely out of date.'

'When did you learn to drive?'

'As soon as I was old enough! Father took great pains to teach me.'

'I'm sure you were a good pupil.' He drove on, and Ann settled herself, glancing at him from time to time as she wondered what it was about him that attracted her.

She could feel a curious lightness in her breast, a sense of happy anticipation which she recalled had filled her during her happier days with Gerry. But surely what she was feeling wasn't anything like love! She wasn't going to fall in love ever again.

The thought scared her for a moment, and she peeped at him, taking in his profile and wondering about him. He was engaged to be married to another girl. She hadn't met him until yesterday, but here she was thinking about falling in love with him.

Confusion attacked her mind and she sat silent, trying to unravel some of the thoughts that whirled in her brain. When she looked at him again she found him glancing at her, and he smiled as their glances met.

'I have an unfair advantage over you,' he said.

'Really?' She wondered what was coming.

'Your mother has told me so much about you that I feel I really know you, and I keep looking at you as if we were friends of long standing. It's disconcerting to realize that I know precious little about you personally.'

'Well there's not much to know!' She smiled as she stared ahead. There were dark clouds in the sky and she thought rain was falling in the distance. But the sun was shining through jagged rents in the clouds, throwing long fingers of pale sunlight to the earth as if probing meticulously for some evidence of life.

'I feel sorry for you! From what your mother said you were to be married.'

Ann smiled, but said nothing.

'It's none of my business,' he went on with a trace of awkwardness filling the background of his voice.

'But you recognize a kindred spirit, is that it?' she demanded.

He stared at her in some surprise, and said nothing. Ann watched his face for a moment. Something was pushing her from inside, some subconscious impulse that demanded to know all there was to learn about him.

'Perhaps I'm being impertinent, but after what happened last night I couldn't help wondering about you. They say you're engaged to be married, but you don't look like a man happily in love.'

'You're too observant,' he said thinly.

'I'm sorry.' She lapsed into silence, but her heart was suddenly pounding again. She was right. He wasn't happily in love. Something had gone wrong with his romance. Did that mean there was a chance for her after all?

'There's nothing to be sorry about. Lot's of people call it off after discovering that it isn't meant for them.' His voice was even, and betrayed no signs of emotion.

'But you haven't called it off, have you?'

He glanced at her and there was a thin smile on his lips. 'You are observant, aren't you? Or was it intuition?'

'I don't know. A little of each, I expect. But you don't want anyone at the Home learning about it, do you?'

'I'm rather sensitive! I'd like to keep it quiet if I can.'

'Well I shan't say anything.' Ann

shook her head as she considered. Her subconscious mind was grasping at the straws which seemed to be coming her way. But she wanted to know why he had changed his mind about marriage. Was it the girl or the whole concept of marriage that had affected him adversely.

They were silent as they went on, and Ann became prey to many impulses. Each passing moment seemed to strengthen the attraction he held for her. She had to keep glancing at him, to take in every detail of his lean, handsome face. His complexion was very fair, his eyes pale blue, and his hair was like wheatstraw. Everything about him found an eager place in her mind, and she was trembling by the time they reached Wentham.

'I'll come with you,' he said as they parked the car, and she did not object.

She felt very elated, walking by his side, and her mind was a playground for every passing fancy. She felt as if she were walking on air, and she couldn't account for the odd impressions floating through her mind. She was acting as if she had come under a spell of some kind, and each passing moment seemed to strengthen her giddiness.

It was the work of a very few minutes to renew her driving licence, and as they walked back to the car Barry smiled at her.

'You can drive me back if you like,' he invited.

'I might have an accident!' She shook her head. 'I'm a woman driver, remember!'

'I had noticed,' he remarked.

Ann tried to call a halt to the mad stampede of thoughts that rioted through her mind. She couldn't understand what was happening to her, and she was beginning to feel afraid that she might make a fool of herself. Already she was acting towards him as if they were friends of long standing, and there was nothing she could do to prevent the feeling from growing ever larger. They reached his car and got into the vehicle, and when his shoulder touched hers, Ann shivered as if an icicle had fallen down her neck.

Rain began to fall and he switched on the windscreen wipers. He glanced at her, his face calm but expressionless, and she smiled slowly, wondering what was passing through his mind. He started the car and glanced around, and she watched him intently, trying to think of something to

109

say, but all of a sudden her mind was a complete blank and she was nervous and tongue tied.

'Straight home?' he asked as he gained the road.

'Is there somewhere else you'd rather go?' she countered, watching his face.

'I do have the afternoon off,' he reminded.

'And you're on duty until midnight, when you start.'

'I don't mind duty at all. It keeps me busy.'

'So there is something in what my mother says. When you're busy you're happy.'

'She's probably right. The days are all the same for me.'

'You sound as if you're very unhappy, and yet when I met you yesterday afternoon I thought you didn't have a care in the world.'

'It's a different matter when I'm out there alone with my painting.' He sighed heavily.

Ann wanted to ask him more, to draw everything from him, but she knew he might resent her interference, and she didn't want to upset him further.

110

'Don't go back to the Home yet if you're not of a mind to do so. I don't have to hurry back!' She spoke quietly, as if she understood his feelings, and he gave her a quickly appreciative smile.

'Thanks! There's a spot I'd like to visit before we do go back. I haven't been there for some time, and I'm in the mood for it.'

'Do I know it?' she asked.

'I expect you do. You're a native of these parts, aren't you?' He was smiling now and his blue eyes seemed alive.

'Born and bred! I hope I never have to move away again.'

'What could possibly make you move away again?'

'I might fall in love again!' Her dark eyes grew round and her tones sounded hollow. 'If I married I'd go where ever my husband wanted to go.'

'I wish I had found a girl like you!'

'Is that the trouble with your romance?'

'Something like that! I don't want to go into details, but she wants to move back to the big city and I'm not keen. Of course, it goes much deeper than that! I'm not in love with her, and I begin to suspect that I never have been. I'm sure she doesn't love me. If she did she wouldn't insist upon such impossible conditions.'

Ann was silent, thinking over his words. It didn't sound as if true love was involved here, she was telling herself. But she would have done anything he'd asked if she had been in his fiancée's shoes.

'I suppose you think I'm an irresponsible fool,' he went on. 'I know I ought to have made my feelings clear to Olive. But I let things drag on and on and she's expecting me to name the date for the wedding. It will also be the date I leave Clover House!'

'And you don't want to go!' Ann nodded her understanding. 'It does seem as if you're in a mess.'

'It's all of that!' He nodded, driving steadily with only half his concentration upon his actions. He glanced at Ann from time to time and she was fully aware of it. 'What would you do if you were in my place?' he demanded. He continued without pause. 'But of course I know what you would do. You must have been faced with a similar situation out there, and you did the right thing.'

'I packed up and came home,' she said, nodding. 'But you can't do that, can you?'

'Not in the same way, but I could make some sort of a decision instead of waffling like an idiot.'

'What does your fiancée think about it? I mean, has she issued you with some kind of an ultimatum?'

'No. She knows I don't like what's happening, but she imagines that I shall fall in line with her desires.'

'That doesn't seem to be the sort of basis I would want in a marriage,' Ann told him boldly.

'How do you mean?'

'It doesn't sound like fifty-fifty to me.'

'You think marriage should be fifty-fifty?'

'Of course? How else could it succeed?'

'What happened to you? Couldn't you get the fifty-fifty basis?'

'It wasn't that. His work seemed more important than any personal life.'

'Ah! I think I know the type.'

'It was my fault really because I ought to have seen it earlier. The signs were plain enough, but I just didn't look for them. I thought everything in the garden was lovely.'

'But you're not hurt by what happened!'

'No! It shows, does it?' Ann smiled as

she glanced at him. 'It was a shock to realize at first that there was not going to be any future for us. But I suppose I had noticed that he was growing away from me all the time, and I just came to accept it.'

'I've got to do something!' Desperation sounded in his voice. 'But I dislike causing trouble of any kind.'

'You'd rather marry her and then live a miserable existence, making her life miserable as well, instead of having it out with her and making a clean break. It may be painful for a bit, but so is having a tooth out. But you get over it after a time.'

'I like your philosophy!' He chuckled, and sounded exactly as he'd sounded the previous afternoon, when Ann had thought him carefree.

'Doesn't she suspect a thing about your true feelings?' Ann persisted.

'I don't think so! Oh, we've never pretended that were madly in love. We're more companionable than anything. I suppose that's an indication that we're not very serious.'

'Well as I see it, you don't have any decision to make.' Ann spoke boldly.

'You're a strange one! I've been worrying over this situation for a long time, but you come along and say there isn't any decision for me to make. Please go on! I'm highly interested to know how you look at it.'

'I would ask myself a simple question.'

'Well I'm listening! Ask yourself the question, then tell me the answer.'

'I'll put the question to you and leave you to find the answer,' she retorted.

'I'm waiting with bated breath.' He was smiling, but she could see that he was serious beneath his banter.

'The question is, would you be happier married to her and living away from Clover House or happier without her and still being the doctor at the Home?'

'You have brought it down to basic problems, haven't you?' He nodded. 'But the answer isn't as simple.'

'I thought it was simply a case of deciding what you wanted most,' Ann said.

'It could well be!' He sighed heavily. 'I must give it some thought.'

'You don't want to reach an agreement,' Ann accused.

'Perhaps you're right! But I don't want to hurt anybody.'

'Have you considered that you might be causing a greater hurt by pretending nothing is wrong?'

'That's true as well! But don't push me! I'll think it over between now and the time we get back to the Home, and I'll come to a decision, one way or the other.'

Ann nodded and settled back, ready to enjoy the ride, and she could not say why she had been so intent upon making him find a solution. But she realized that she wanted him to break with this unknown fiancée! The knowledge was large and very plain in her mind. What she didn't know yet was the reason behind her motives. As they went on during the afternoon she tried to puzzle it out, and the only thing that became clear was that she liked Barry Lander's company much more than had ever cared for Gerry's.

Chapter Six

Ann quickly settled back home, and the days went by in rapid succession. Before she could hardly grasp the fact, the first weekend was over and she was preparing to start working as a nurse. She was going on duty from two until ten for five days, and as her first afternoon tour of duty approached she began to look forward to it with increasing pleasure.

She found herself helping out on the ground floor, under Sister Corbin's supervision, and there were twenty-two patients on the floor to be taken care of. Walking around the corridors dressed in her uniform, Ann felt that she had really broken all contact with the past, and her pleasure increased when she saw Barry Lander in her father's company, coming to examine a patient.

'Hello,' Frank Bowman said. 'It seems we have a new nurse at work here. How do you like it, Nurse?'

'Very well, thank you, Doctor!' Ann

117

smiled as she continued on her way, but she let her gaze linger a little on Barry. Since their afternoon driving together she hadn't found the opportunity to talk to him alone, and she was aching to know what decision he had reached about his future.

He smiled lightly at her, but said nothing, and she felt a bit crestfallen as she continued. Her feelings for him had hardened considerably during the weekend, and she found herself now with definite hopes of getting to know him better.

The only black spot she had encountered since her arrival home was Hugh Leighton who insisted upon taking her out on Saturday evening. By the time they had parted she knew she was going to have trouble with Hugh, and she had been trying to think of some way to let him know for certain that she could never care for him. But all her mental energies were taken up by thoughts of Barry, and nothing else seemed to matter now.

Sister Corbin appeared in the office doorway, and she seemed startled as Ann walked straight past her instead of turning in at the office.

'Are you looking for me, by any chance,

Ann?' Sister Corbin demanded, and Ann dragged herself back to the present to find her superior staring at her with a puzzled expression on her good natured face. 'My word! You were far from here! Not back where you came from, were you?'

'No!' Ann shook her head as she smiled. 'I'm sorry about that. I'm not usually given to wool-gathering. What can I do now?'

'Just keep an eye on things generally. The visitors will be coming in at two-thirty, and when they arrive you'll have your work cut out filling vases for the flowers they bring, and making sure that the patients don't receive anything that's prohibited on dietary grounds. You'd be surprised at some of the things visitors bring in. And if anyone asks you how the patients are, refer them to me. I shall be in my office most of the afternoon.'

Ann nodded and began to move on, but Sister Corbin put a hand on her arm.

'We've got a few minutes before things hot up, Ann. Let's have a chat. Come into the office. You've seen the indicator board. If anyone wants anything they ring for us.'

Ann nodded, and followed her superior into the office. She was wondering what was on Sister Corbin's mind, and stared into the woman's face as she awaited some intimation.

'It's none of my business, Ann, but I saw you out with Hugh Leighton on Saturday.'

'I didn't know you knew Hugh!'

'Well I've been here several years now. I know he's an old friend of yours, but are you aware that he's practically engaged to a girl who lives in York?'

'No!' Ann's face showed genuine surprise. 'Are you sure?'

'I know the girl!'

'But this is wonderful!'

Sister Corbin looked a bit surprised, and Ann smiled.

'I've spent the rest of the week end trying to think up some reason for telling Hugh I don't want to see him again. This girl in York is the perfect reason.'

'Then you're not interested in Hugh!' There was relief in the Sister's voice.

'I never have been! I could have married Hugh years ago if I'd wanted him!' Ann felt relief surging through her mind. 'He's the same old Hugh, though. I can remember when he threw over a very good friend of mine in the hope of catching me, but it didn't work, and he never went back to her. I feel sorry for this girl in York, though, if she's in love with Hugh. He'll never settle down.'

'You don't mind me bringing this up?' Sister Corbin demanded.

'Not at all! I'm glad you did. It's given me something to work on.'

'I knew you didn't know the exact situation. But then again, you and Hugh are very old friends.'

'Don't worry about it. I know Hugh very well.' Ann was relieved by what she had learned. She pictured Hugh's face and nodded slowly. He had been most insistent over the week end, and she'd been hard put to keep him at bay. But now she had the perfect answer to him.

The afternoon passed very quickly, especially when the visitors arrived, and Ann was kept busy until tea time. She lost count of the times she hurried along the corridor, fetching vases, hurrying into the kitchen for water, arranging flowers, going from room to room to check on the patients and the visitors, and by the time she settled into her work the visitors had to leave. Her legs were aching as she went along the corridor checking that the visitors were departing, and when order was restored at last she heaved a long sigh of relief and went to report to Sister Corbin.

'What an afternoon!' she declarerd, and her superior looked up from her reports with a slow smile spreading across her face. 'I don't think I can walk another step! I haven't been on the go so much since I worked in a general hospital years ago.'

'It isn't very often like this,' came the gentle reply. 'But we do get odd moments of madness.'

'It's time to start getting teas out, isn't it?' Ann was still filled with enthusiasm.

'The maids will be arriving shortly. Nurse Dermot will be in the kitchen now. If you go along she'll show you what needs to be done.'

Ann nodded and set out for the kitchen, but on the way she met Barry Lander. He was coming along the corridor, a chart in his hand, and his face showed her that he was deep in thought. She had to step out of his path, and he looked up at her, startled by her quick movement.

'It's lucky you were not driving your car at that moment,' she observed slowly.

'Oh! I'm sorry! I was miles away. I

don't know what's coming over me! But no harm done! How are you settling down to work?'

'My legs are protesting, but otherwise I'm coping.'

'I expect you'll get used to it.' He sounded subdued, and there was wistfulness in his expression. His eyes seemed too bright for the dull afternoon, and Ann felt her heart swell as she tried to control the sudden rush of emotion which came over her. 'You're a very capable person.'

'Are you still worried by that problem you mentioned the other night?' she asked boldly, and he firmed his lips.

'Naturally I'm on edge about it. I haven't reached a decision yet, although I know I'd be far unhappier away from here than I would be married to Olive!' He smiled thinly.

'So what's the problem?' Ann tried to keep her tones even and sympathetic. 'But of course, you don't want to hurt her. But it could prove to be the wrong attitude, as I pointed out. You could hurt her a lot more by marrying her and postponing the inevitable revelation.'

He was nodding slowly. 'It's refreshing to talk to you,' he admitted. 'You make everything seem so easy. Your outlook on life is rather clinical.'

'Well what do you expect from a nurse?' she demanded lightly.

He smiled, but shook his head, and Ann clenched her teeth as she felt her emotions rise. His face was stuck in her mind and she was beginning to dream about him. How could she settle down to this routine, exacting as it was, while he was around, upsetting her with the merest smile or glance? What had she come home to? Nothing was going to turn out the way she planned. She had spent three years mentally suffering the situation into which she had plunged so hopefully, and now she was home and hoping that her life would run more happily and he was here, startling her and making her wonder why he could make her so uneasy and restless.

'Now you're miles away,' he said, his voice jerking her free of her thoughts. 'What's on your mind? Or are you not so clinical and decisive as I imagine? Are you hiding anything?'

'I don't think so!' She smiled as she imagined what his attitude would be if she told him that she had been instantly attracted to him and was now fondly imagining that she was in love with him. She was startled by the revelation! It had come unbidden into her mind, and she knew her face was showing something of her feelings. She tried to compose herself instantly but failed, and while he looked into her eyes she was staring at him with all her secrets bared in her expression.

'I'd like to talk to you some more,' he said, and she was relieved that he couldn't read what was showing in her face.

'I don't get finished until ten!'

'What about tomorrow morning? You're off duty until two. I have the morning off.'

'All right. Where shall we talk?'

'If the sun is shining tomorrow, and the weather forecast is good, I believe, then I shall do some painting down at the brook. If you'd care to walk that way we could talk.'

'Wouldn't I disturb your work?' she demanded.

'I can leave that for a bit.'

'All right. What time will you be there?'

'About ten.' There was sudden hope in his voice, and Ann felt her mind expanding as she encompassed the new impressions flowing through it.

'And if it rains?' She tried to discard the probability.

'Then perhaps we could go for a short drive.'

She smiled and nodded. 'All right, but it wouldn't do for us to leave here together, would it? After all, you are engaged to be married, and I'm not your fiancée!' Her words faltered a little, and she tried to renew her hold upon her emotions.

'I'm sure no one would read anything wrong into our going out together.'

'Except your fiancée!'

'Perhaps you're right.' There was sudden doubt in his voice, and Ann was worried that she'd gone too far. She wanted to go out with him. The knowledge was large in her mind, and she was finding it difficult to resist the impulse to tell him so.

'Well perhaps it won't rain,' she said quickly. 'No one can say anything if we happen to meet down by the brook.'

His smile rewarded her, and she sighed with relief. She heard him sigh, and then they parted and went their separate ways.

Ann was most thoughtful as she helped Nurse Dermot prepare tea for the patients. There were diets to be prepared, and Nurse Dermot had a list for reference.

Ann soon showed that she was a great help, and they chatted as they worked.

'Are you happy to be back here and working, Ann?' Effie Dermot asked. Her red hair was almost completely hidden under her cap, but strands of it glinted around her ears, and her sea-green eyes were liquid and expressive.

'I'm very happy now,' Ann agreed. 'There's such a nice atmosphere. Perhaps it's only my imagination, seeing that my parents run and own the place, but I've never come across a better run or happier nursing home.'

'I'll agree with that. I'm very happy here. It would break my heart to have to leave.' Effie spoke seriously, and Ann looked into the girl's beautiful eyes.

'You're not thinking of leaving, are you?'

'It has crossed my mind.'

'Is anything wrong?' Ann was immediately ready to help.

'Nothing wrong, but I have considered leaving.'

'What ever for?'

'I'd better not say. You'd think me a complete fool if I told you about it.' Effie returned her full concentration to cutting bread and buttering it, and the breadknife flashed in her expert hands.

'If there's anything I can help with then don't hesitate to tell me. I certainly wouldn't think you any kind of a fool. We all get problems to overcome at different times in our lives, you know.'

'That's true. It wouldn't be life if everything was plain sailing.'

'Perhaps you'll tell me about it when you get to know me better,' Ann suggested.

'It isn't that we're practically strangers! I can tell that you're one of the best. You're naturally sympathetic, just like Matron. But this is something I'd never dare tell a living soul.'

'It sounds mysterious, but don't tell me about it if you think I can't help.'

'I'm in love with someone who doesn't even know I exist,' the girl said slowly, her eyes downcast, and Ann saw her hands were trembling.

'That is a problem,' she said instantly. 'I can't imagine anything worse in this world.'

'The trouble is, he's in love with someone else, so there can never be any hope for me. I've thought about going away from here in an attempt to forget all about him. But it's like torture if I don't see him at all.'

'Oh! That does make it a mountain-sized problem.' Ann shook her head, her face showing sympathy as Effie glanced sideways at her.

'Do you think I'm just an idiot?' the girl demanded.

'Certainly not. A girl can't help falling in love, and she can't always choose the man she loves. It happens sometimes that love strikes in the most unexpected places.' Her tones quivered a little as she thought of Barry, and a sigh escaped her despite her efforts to contain it.

'That's how I've looked at it. I've been hoping that a miracle would happen and that he'd part from his fiancée, but it isn't the age for miracles any more. I'm just wasting my time, I know it, but I'm one of the world's eternal optimists, and I keep on waiting and hoping.'

'Haven't you tried to go out and find someone you could like? It isn't easy, I know, but if another man attracted you then you'd soon forget this one.'

'I've tried that, but I cringe when I come up against someone else.'

Everyone seems to have problems, Ann

was thinking. She let her mind encompass Barry once more, and thought of his problem. But he could so easily clear himself. His indecision stemmed from the fact that he didn't want to cause the girl any distress. He wouldn't admit that by lingering as he was doing he could make her unhappiness greater.

They parted to go about their duties then, and Ann didn't get the opportunity to talk to Effie for some time. But she carried the girl's problems in her mind, and wished she could help. But the kind of help that Effie needed was outside Ann's scope.

When teas had been served and the cleaning up which followed had been dealt with, Ann went for her own break, and she didn't go along to the staff dining room but took care of her own food in their private wing. She sat down to a plate of food, and had just commenced the meal when her mother appeared.

'Hello, dear, how did you get on today?' Mrs Bowman enquired. 'I'm sorry I didn't get the chance to see you during the afternoon, but I'm sure you managed quite well.'

'The time went rather quickly,' Ann

130

replied. 'Have you finished duty for the day?'

'I have. But you're on duty until ten, aren't you?' Mrs Bowman sat down at the table and watched Ann for some moments. 'I've had a most pleasant afternoon myself. I was busy with the visitors, but each time I got a free moment I told myself that you were doing your duty here. You can't imagine how nice that made me feel.'

'So you've really been missing me!' Ann smiled thoughtfully as she looked at her mother. 'Well I've missed you just as much, although perhaps I haven't realized it until now. It's really wonderful to be back, and I never want to go away again as long as I live.'

'Do you think you'll settle down to this quieter life without trouble?'

'I've already settled down! This is my home, Mother! I don't have to settle down here again. It comes naturally, like putting on a nurse's uniform.'

'I can't help worrying about you, Ann. You need happiness in this world as well as satisfaction. You can't tell me you weren't hurt at all by this change of situation you've experienced.'

'I can tell you, and I will.' Ann looked

into her mother's eyes. 'That's the strange thing about it all. I never had a moment's heartache. That's the truth, Mother. I wouldn't lie to you.'

'Then you got off very lightly, but no doubt the experience will frighten you away from making contact with someone else.'

'I don't think so!' Ann's eyes gleamed for a moment, and she was thinking of Barry. 'If the right man comes along there'll be nothing I can do about it. That's the way of life, isn't it?'

'That's certainly the way it goes. I don't want to push you into the arms of another man, but I don't want to see you grow up into a dedicated nurse with no personal emotions. I've seen that happen too many times to a lot of good nurses, Ann. Usually they come across just such a situation that faces you, and they turn their backs upon men and dedicate themselves to nursing. They all end up very skilled in their work, and very lonely.'

'Well I'm not going out deliberately to find someone to take Gerry's place.' Ann smiled. 'I told you, if the right man comes along then I'll be ready for him.'

She continued with her meal, aware that she had only thirty minutes before having to report back on duty. She was filled with a joy that showed clearly in her eyes. This was where she belonged, and her heart told her so in quite plain language.

When she went back on duty she was thoughtful. Effie departed on her break, and Sister Corbin appeared and gave her several tasks to do. But it was when she came into contact with the patients that she found the greatest pleasure, and she answered all the calls for attention with alacrity as soon as the indicator board buzzed its warning.

Hurrying to answer one such summons, Ann found herself standing in a doorway and looking at a man lying in the bed in the room. She hadn't been to this particular room before, and when the man turned his gaze from the window, where evening was beginning to draw its shadows across the grounds, he stiffened a little, then smiled.

'Hello,' he said cheerfully. 'A new nurse! And a beautiful one at that!' He had an American accent, and it caressed Ann's ears as she walked to the foot of his bed and glanced at his chart.

'Hello, Mr Oakley,' she said, smiling.

'I'm Nurse Bowman. What can I do for you?'

'Bowman! That's a common name around here. Have you got a few moments to talk to me, Nurse? Are you kin to Matron and Doctor Bowman?'

'They're my parents. I can't stay long because the other nurse is having her meal break and I have to sit in the office in case of calls.'

'I see. Well I have heard about you. So you're Ann Bowman. No wonder your mother is proud of you. She's told me a lot about you.'

'I try to live up to her high ideals,' Ann replied.

'I'm sure you do!' He was a heavily built man, dark and strongly handsome. His chart gave his age as twenty-five. His rugged face had an American look about it. 'Look, I don't want to be a bother to you or any of the nurses, but I'd like some reading material.'

'What sort of material would you care for?'

'Something historical! I was a free lance journalist in America before I went to work on the oil rigs. I like Yorkshire. It's rich in tradition and history, and

134

I'd like to write some articles about it. Is there anything historical in this place? There ought to be. It's got quite a lot of history behind it.'

'Are you permitted to work?' Ann asked.

'No. I've got something wrong with my heart and I've got to rest. That's okay as far as my physical self is concerned, but I think my mental outlook should be catered for as well.'

'Perhaps I'd better have a word with the doctor,' she began, and he shook his head and grimaced.

'That won't do any good. He's a hard man! I'm trapped here in this bed whether I like it or not. Sure he's gonna try and cure me. That's what I came here for. But I sure wish I could do something constructive to pass the time. I might get out of here in a couple of months with a good heart again, but by the time I do I shall be plain nuts.'

Ann could not help smiling, but she nodded sympathetically.

'I'll have a word with the doctor about you, Mr Oakley,' she said. 'It's the best I can do. Under the treatment you're having, things like reading and writing are regarded as detrimental to your recovery. If you're not allowed books then it's really for your own good.'

'I know! You're going to cure me even if you have to kill me to do so.' He chuckled lightly. 'Thanks, Nurse, for listening so sympathetically, but forget about asking the doctor. I know what his answer will be.'

Ann stared at him for a moment. 'Don't you have any visitors?' she demanded.

'It's a long way from the States!'

'Then you don't have your family over here with you!'

'Not yet! It'll be a month or two before they can get here.'

'Well if there's anything I can do for you then let me know.'

'That's kind of you. When you're off duty you could come and talk to me for a spell. I get kind of lonely lying here with no one to talk to. You nurses have too much to do while you're on duty, and I guess that would go for the doctor as well.'

'All right, Mr Oakley, I'll come and talk to you, and I will have a word with my father to see if there's something you can do to occupy your mind.'

He nodded, and Ann departed back to the office, to find the indicator board buzzing madly and three indicators flickering for attention. Noting the room numbers, Ann hurried in answer, and she was kept busy until Effie Dermot returned to duty. Then they settled down for the evening, and more visitors arrived.

Ann found no time for herself until she went off duty. But she was well pleased with her work, and felt satisfied as she went back to the private wing, tired and aching in every muscle. Yet if all her days proved as fruitful then she knew she would have no regrets, and she went to bed happy in the knowledge that at last her life seemed to be justified. She could ask for no more than that!

Chapter Seven

Next morning Ann prepared to go and meet Barry down at the brook, and she was elated as she saw that the morning was fine, although a sharp breeze was blowing. At the appointed time she left the Home and wended her way out to the footpath, and she glanced around as if afraid that she might be seen. But nothing happened to prevent her keeping the rendezvous, and as she neared the bridge and saw Barry's tall figure there her heart seemed to give a double-beat.

He was staring moodily into the ruffled surface of the water, and Ann sensed the loneliness and low spirits that held him. It was apparent that he had not reached a favourable conclusion in his problems, and she shook her head slowly as she considered. He didn't see her until she had almost reached him, and she had the opportunity to study his downcast features. She found a great deal of emotion for him in her mind, and as she reached his side she tried to keep her mind clear. She was becoming involved with him, and although that wasn't against her will she knew she had no resistance at all.

'Hello!' She spoke softly, and he started, his thoughts far away.

'Hello!' His voice was throaty, low pitched. But his expression cleared as he collected himself and smiled. 'It was good of you to come.'

'Not at all! I need some fresh air. I'm a working girl again, and I'm the type who doesn't bother to get out and about when I'm off duty.' She glanced around at the familiar scene, and thought the views had never looked better. There was a leaping eagerness inside her which could hardly be contained, and she knew her eyes must be shining and her cheeks filled with colour. She felt elated, and realized it would show.

He smiled gently, and turned to walk along the path that led around Clover Farm. Ann fell into step beside him, aware that she was supremely happy.

'I thought you were going to paint this morning,' she remarked.

'It's too windy! In any case, I don't feel in the mood. I thought perhaps you wouldn't mind walking for a bit.'

'All right!' She nodded her agreement, and experienced a thrill of relief as they wandered on.

They passed the farm, and Ann was on tenterhooks until they were out of sight of it in case they should see her uncle or her cousin. But they escaped detection, and she began to revel in his company as they went on along the footpath that meandered across the broad patchwork of fields. It was a public footpath, but it was deserted at this time. Ann was beside herself with happiness. She kept glancing at him, watching his expressions, wondering about him, and telling herself that she had never spent a more comfortable time with any man.

He seemed to possess a kind of magic that smoothed away all her intentions of remaining aloof and remote from men. After her experiences abroad she had vowed to live an uneventful life, but here she was thrilled at being in his company and already looking on the bright side despite the fact that he had a fiancée.

Barry said little as they continued, and she was content merely to be in his company. Each passing minute seemed to add a little to the joy in her heart, and try as she might, she could not pull herself up from the path along which her mind seemed intent upon travelling. Here was a man who interested her deeply, who seemed to captivate her with intangible powers such as she had never before experienced, and she was already thinking that perhaps they had been destined to meet and fall in love. Even the fact that he was engaged to be married didn't seem to matter. Ordinarily she wouldn't have looked at any man twice with the knowledge that he was engaged, but this was different. She seemed to have lost her senses completely.

'It's good of you to give up your morning like this,' Barry said at length. 'I know I have quite a nerve asking you to come along, but you're such a good hearted and friendly girl that I was automatically drawn to you as soon as we met.'

She nodded slowly, aware that she had suffered the same symptoms, and his words seemed to strengthen her conviction that they had been intended to meet long before she had come home.

'I like you,' she said with no trace of awkwardness. 'If I can help you then I will. But you've got to get over your indecisiveness and put these matters right.'

'I did that yesterday!' He glanced sideways at her, no doubt wondering how she was going to accept the news, but Ann did not permit her wild sense of relief from his words to leap into her expression.

'You told your fiancée?' she repeated slowly.

'Yes! I knew I couldn't put it off any longer.'

'How did she take it?'

'Better than I expected. She seemed to be relieved. She said she knew we weren't suited all along, and she rather hoped I would come to this decision.'

'Then it wasn't such an ordeal after all!' Ann sighed deeply as a knot of tension departed from her mind.

'It wasn't.' He smiled as he glanced at her, a secret little smile that made her wonder what was going through his mind.

'Then why are you so wistful this morning?'

'There is still one problem facing me.'

'Is it something I can help with?'

'I don't know what you would think if I

told you about it.' He paused and looked at her. Ann watched his face, taking in his fleeting emotions, and she felt a pang of intuition.

The breeze blew in her face and twitched her dark hair. The sun was bright but without warmth, and it was a sign that summer was gone. Most of the fields were bare now, with the harvest in, and already some work was going on to prepare for next year's crops. She looked into his face, noting the sharpness in his blue eyes, and in that silent moment she could almost read his thoughts.

'I'm beginning to wonder what kind of a man I am,' he went on. 'I became engaged to marry a girl I didn't love, and I've broken off that engagement because I'm in love with someone else.'

His words shocked Ann like a slapped face. She gasped and stared at him, totally surprised by what he had said.

'Well!' She could say nothing else, and her dark eyes were narrowed as she regarded his face.

'I feel caught up in the coils of some strange spell,' he went on. 'I just don't know what's happening to me.'

'Were you in love with this other girl

before you became engaged, or did you meet her afterwards and then discover that you had no love for your fiancée?'

'I knew I wasn't in love with my fiancée before this other girl came into my life.' He spoke steadily, patiently, and when Ann glanced at him she saw he was staring away across the fields, his pale eyes filled with brightness.

There was a pain in her own heart, and she felt stifled by her conflicting emotions. It seemed that she was wrong in her surmise that they had been meant for each other! She tried to close her mind to the torment which tried to break through into her consciousness. She had snatched at what she imagined was a fateful chance, but she had erred, and she would have to face that fact.

'They say true love makes itself felt immediately,' she retorted, and now the day seemed to have taken on a deeper shadow.

'Then I have found my true love,' he retorted gravely.

She nodded slowly, her own dreams fading quickly, and she began to see the foolishness in her wishful thinking. She had expected to come home and walk straight into another man's arms, and her romantic dreams had been doomed to failure from the outset. Her experiences abroad ought to have warned her that true love was not for her. She was going to become one of those maiden nurses her mother spoke against.

'A great many people never have the chance of meeting their true loves,' she said seriously. 'It's a dreadful thing to think that two people can live out their whole lives without finding their soul mates.'

'Do you believe in that sort of thing?'

'Yes, I think I do, although I've always tried to remain practicable.'

'And you've never found your true love?'

'That's fairly obvious!' She smiled thinly as she glanced at him. 'But I wish you luck. It's nice to hear that someone has found what he's been looking for.'

'But it isn't as simple as that,' he went on. 'I know she's my soul mate, as you called it, but she doesn't know I exist.'

'Then you've got to let her know somehow!'

'I expected you to say that.' His voice suddenly became more friendly, and Ann suppressed a sigh as she looked into his blue eyes. His manner seemed more at ease, and she wondered who the lucky girl was. 'But can I tell her right out of the blue, just like that?' he demanded.

'I don't know of a better way.' Ann smiled, telling herself that some lucky girl was going to get the surprise of her life. 'If she is your soul mate then she'll know it deep inside and she'll respond.'

He nodded slowly. 'That's the way I was looking at it, but if she isn't my soul mate then she's going to laugh at me and I'll be sunk without trace.'

'You've got nothing to lose. If you don't speak up she may turn to someone else.'

'I would lose hope if she turned me down, and hope is what most of us cling to these days.'

'Faint heart never won fair lady!' she quoted.

'I can't argue with that!' A smile touched his lips, and she felt her pulses race as she saw it. Everything about his face seemed to fit in with her ideas of a dream man. It was uncanny how she had come to think of him as a friend of long standing. But he was pushing her into a nightmare with his talk of being in love with someone else. For a few moments she had been on top of the world. He had declared that his engagement was broken off! That had seemed to clear the way for her, but now there was someone else.

'I hope you won't be disappointed,' she said. 'You'll be very fortunate indeed if you do secure true love.'

'It's a gamble,' he agreed. They were walking alongside a narrow river, and sunlight sparkled upon the still water. The utter peacefulness got right into Ann's soul, and she was filled with joy despite her upset mind. But she held her higher feelings at bay as she looked at him and wished that she could be his sweetheart. At this moment in time it was all she could wish for.

'Don't let your opportunities slip by,' she warned. 'If you want anything in this world then you've got to grasp it with both hands.'

'All right!' There was sudden determination in his tones. He stopped walking and turned to her, and Ann halted and looked up into his face. 'I've only known you a few days,' he said, his voice sharp. 'But from the very first moment I felt something for you in my mind. I can't explain it, but in the very few days since that first time

I've come to the conclusion that I've fallen in love with you.'

In the silence that followed, Ann felt that her heart and pulses had stopped. She felt stifled, and when she tried to open her mouth to speak she discovered that all her muscles had become momentarily paralysed. Barry said nothing. He stood motionless, watching her intently and awaiting her reaction. His eyes were wide and filled with brightness, and Ann struggled mentally to overcome her surprise. But already there was a fierce joy speeding through her mind. Yet she was afraid to accept the evidence of her ears.

'I can see that I've shocked you.' He smiled slowly. 'But I'm only following your advice.'

She nodded, unable yet to speak, and then she took a deep breath and held it, feeling animation running once more through her body.

'I'm flabbergasted!' she admitted.

'I'm sorry! I ought to have kept it to myself.' There was a trace of bitterness in his voice. 'What kind of a fool am I? You've just returned home after a bad expedition into the world of romance, and straightway I throw this at you. I've placed you in an unenviable position. You'll never be able to look at me without recalling this moment, and when you've had time to get over the shock I've given you then you'll wonder what on earth possessed me to speak like this.'

'I think I know what possessed you,' Ann said slowly. 'You see, the same sort of thing overcame me almost as soon as I saw you.'

It was his turn to show surprise, but Ann saw also the light of hope which came into his blue eyes. Twice he tried to speak, but he was held speechless by the same kind of shock that had held her. Ann smiled slowly.

'So I've got my own back on you,' she said. 'But it's true! I think I fell in love with you at first sight!'

He reached out and took hold of her hands, still unable to speak, and Ann felt her pulses begin to race in an exquisite manner. She moistened her lips, and her shoulders lifted as she suppressed a sigh.

'I'm wondering if I'm trying sub-consciously to get over the disappointment I felt out there,' she said softly. 'It was a disappointment after so many years of hoping, but I'm glad everything fell through as it did. I wasn't in love with Gerry at the end, and although I believed myself to be in love with him at first, I've had the knowledge that it wasn't love, and it's been quite strong since I met you.'

'Do you think two people can fall in love at first sight?' He sounded hopeful, and smiled when she nodded.

'It's happened to us, hasn't it?' she countered.

'I think so. I know I feel strangely about you. I haven't been able to sleep since I met you.'

'And I've been bewildered by you!' She smiled slowly. 'It's quite cold blooded too, isn't it? That's what makes me think it must be love.'

'May I kiss you?' he asked softly.

'Yes!' She bated her breath as she tensed, and he slowly put his arms around her shoulders.

In the moment that their lips met, Ann felt as if the earth had stopped revolving. She closed her eyes at their contact and felt her senses spin giddily. Elation filled her. She put her arms about him and returned his kiss with all her heart, and when they finally moved apart they were both breathless. They looked into each other's eyes, and Ann read his expression and knew he was affected as much by her as she was by him.

'That has proved something,' he said at length.

'It did to me!' Her dark eyes were filled with fervour as she watched his expression. 'I wasn't disappointed.'

'And neither was I!' He shook his head. 'What's happening to us? This isn't the way a romance should be conducted.'

'I've got no complaints!' She smiled easily and he nodded seriously as he watched her.

'All my tensions have gone. What do you suppose happened to us?'

'I don't think we'll ever know. One short week has wrought so much change that I can hardly consider what went on before!' Ann was serious as she faced up to him. His expression showed that he was thinking along the same lines, and he nodded slowly.

'I'd heard so much about you from your mother that I felt I knew you long before you came home.'

'That might explain your feelings now, but I didn't know you existed until I arrived home!'

He took hold of her arm and walked her on, and Ann felt so many wonderful emotions fleeting across her consciousness that she was quite unable to contain them all. Her hands trembled and her heart seemed to race. She had thought she'd known love with Gerry, but what was happening now proved to her beyond all doubt that Gerry had been as nothing. He'd been a very close friend, but nothing more.

They walked on along the meandering path, and time seemed to have lost all significance, until Barry glanced at his watch and whistled softly.

'We're going to be late for duty if we don't turn back now,' he observed.

'I don't want to go back,' Ann retorted. 'I could walk on like this for the rest of my life.'

He smiled as he swung around to face the way they had come. The fields encompassed them, isolating them from the rest of the world, and no matter where they looked, they failed to spot another human being.

'I'm going to remember this morning for the rest of my life,' Ann said softly as they started retracing their steps.

'And I'll certainly never forget it,' he retorted. 'I really don't know what to think yet, Ann! The last few days have been pure torture. Every time I talked to you I seemed to sink deeper and deeper into this strange situation, until I had to do something about it. But don't let me push you into anything! My enthusiasm might conceivably fire your own feelings falsely. I wouldn't want that to happen.'

'Then perhaps we'd better try to be less intense for a bit.' She scanned his face and saw approval in his pale blue eyes. 'I really don't know if I'm on my head or my heels.'

They walked on in silence for some moments, and Ann was considering the events of the morning. What had happened surpassed even her wildest dreams. When he had dropped his bombshell about being in love with yet another woman she had felt the bottom dropping out of her world, but now she knew she was that other woman she could scarcely contain herself. It all seemed too good to be true, and when she glanced at him and saw pleasure in his countenance she realized that it was not just an overwhelming dream but the absolute truth. He had fallen in love with her at first sight. Her own sweet feelings were reciprocated.

At times it seemed to Ann that she was walking on air. She felt Barry's strong arm about her waist and marvelled at it. Now she was certain that they had been fated for each other. No two people could ever have come together in this fashion without realizing that they were meant for one another! She sighed deeply, her mind churning over and over with the most promising hopes she'd ever held.

But a note of caution began to spread through her when they came at last in sight of the Home. Reality swirled down about them again and Barry let go of her, now walking sedately at her side. As they crossed the little bridge over the brook he paused and looked round.

'I shall never forget that day you came here for the first time,' he said softly. 'You were completely lost in thought and I sat watching you for a long time, afraid to betray my presence because I knew it would dispel your thoughts. I recognized you immediately from the photographs your mother has of you, and I didn't think any girl could appear so beautiful. I felt a sudden longing in that first moment which is still with me, and I don't suppose I shall ever lose it now.'

She smiled up at him, enjoying the softness of his face. His hands touched her shoulders reassuringly, and a sigh shuddered through her as she recalled her own feelings on that first day. The world had seemed to gain an extra quality then. The very sight of him had gilded her entire outlook. She had changed immediately inside, and her longings had spread quickly until they emphasized the fact that he was a most extraordinary man!

'I had never been more startled in my life when you spoke to me,' she admitted slowly. 'And when I saw you I knew instinctively that you were going to become important to me. I remember meeting you in the woods after it had started raining, when you were sheltering under that tree. I was filled with so much emotion at just standing beside you! I don't pretend to understand it, Barry, and I don't want to question it.'

'There's no need to ask any questions,' he replied, putting a hand gently upon her shoulder. 'After these revelations we must give ourselves time to get used to one another. You may have second thoughts, you know.'

'Not me!' she said fervently, and he smiled and hugged her.

But they had to part, and they entered the Home and went their different ways. Ann felt sharp pangs of hunger within, and was greatly surprised to discover that she was due to go on duty in something less than an hour. She tried to pull herself up short mentally and square her mind for seeing her parents, but there was a heat in her cheeks which warned her they were flushed, and her eyes were smarting with emotion.

She was unfortunate to meet both her parents at lunch, unfortunate, she thought, because she was certain they could read her mind, if not her expression.

'I was getting worried about you, Ann,' Mrs Bowman said, while Ann's father subjected her to a close scrutiny.

'I went for a walk, and I rather lost myself in the scenery. It's been a long time since I enjoyed myself as much.'

'The wind has put colour into your cheeks,' Frank Bowman said with a faint smile. The expression on his face was both knowing and comforting. 'You were always keen on the great outdoors, Ann!'

'It was a perfect morning for rambling,' Ann retorted.

'Did you see Barry anywhere on your travels?' Mrs Bowman asked.

'As a matter of fact I did. I met him down by the brook. He was walking, so I accompanied him.'

She thought her voice gave her away, despite the fact that she'd tried to keep her tones casual. She saw her parents exchange glances, and she pretended not to notice, although she felt awkward and guilty in front of them.

'You had a telephone call this morning,' Mrs Bowman said.

'Oh?' Ann hardly dared to meet her mother's keen gaze. 'Who called?'

'Hugh Leighton! He wants you to call him!'

'Hugh knows I'm on duty all this week. But I'll call him.' Ann began to eat the meal her mother set before her. 'I want to have a chat with you about one of the patients, Father,' she said hurriedly, wanting to change the situation. 'It's about Mr Oakley. He was asking me yesterday for something to read. What's the ruling on that?'

'I'm afraid he must not exert himself for several weeks to come,' her father replied, nodding. 'I meant to have a word with you about him, in case he tried to get you to take him some reading matter. If we're not very careful with him we might lose him.'

'You mean he might die?' Ann demanded.

'That's it exactly!' Frank Bowman nodded. 'Do what you can to ease his mind, Ann, but keep the truth away from him.'

'Poor man! He seems so ruggedly strong.'

'You can't always go by appearances,' Mrs Bowman said. 'But let's leave shop talk for when we're on duty. It occupies ninety-nine percent of our lives as it is. I want to talk to you, Ann, about Barry. You know he's engaged to be married, don't you?'

'I have been told,' Ann replied, nodding. She didn't feel ready to talk about Barry, and she realized that she could not confide in her mother about the events of morning. She had a strange feeling now that nothing had really happened after all, that it was all wishful thinking. Two people couldn't fall in love just like that! Then her instincts took over and she knew it wasn't just a wonderful dream. It had happened all right, and there would be other times as well, to remind her. She hoped all her future mornings could be as happy as today. Then she would never be less than joyful. But she sensed that she had to keep all this to herself for the time being. Other people probably wouldn't understand what had happened, and Ann felt that she didn't want to share anything yet!

Chapter Eight

The days began to pass more quickly after Ann settled into the routine of the nursing home, and soon she came to know the patients under her care and to learn all about them. In two weeks she began to feel as if she'd never been away from home, and she settled down into a comfortable life that promised everything. The second week found her going on duty at six in the morning until two in the afternoon, and this suited her because she was free in the evenings when Barry was off duty.

Her relationship with Barry plunged on at breath-taking speed. There was no lagging period where they had to get to know one another. They both felt as if they'd known each other for years, and Barry could not help repeating the fact whenever they were together.

They did not leave the home together when they went out. Ann didn't like deceiving anyone, but she felt it better to keep everything secret for a while longer.

Most of the staff imagined that Barry was still engaged to be married, and he didn't feel like broadcasting the facts of his private life. But they got together whenever they were off duty. Ann would drive off in her mother's car and wait in a convenient lay-by for Barry to arrive. They would lock one of the cars and leave it while they went off in the other. In that way Ann managed to keep the truth from her mother, and she was very pleased with the way things were going.

One black spot in her life became obvious as the days went by. Hugh Leighton began to pester her with telephone calls, despite the fact that she told him she knew about his fiancée. Hugh denied he was officially engaged, and said he would rather marry Ann than anyone else. But she refused to go out with him again, and he had to content himself with telephoning at odd times and trying to keep her in a state of indecision.

Then Petra Grahame telephoned during one afternoon just after Ann had come off duty. Ann hadn't seen the girl since she'd called on her that first evening home and they had gone to Hugh's party. But as soon as she discovered it was Petra on the line,

Ann gave the customary excuse of having been too busy for anything but duty.

'I know you're busy, Ann, but I must have you at my party on Saturday. If you're doing the six till two shift then you'll be free on Saturday. Please say you'll come.'

Ann thought of Hugh, and guessed he would also be at the party. Then she thought of Barry, and wanted to be in his company on Saturday evening. But she didn't want to take him to the party.

'Let me think about it, Petra, and I'll call you later,' she said at length.

'I'd like you to agree now,' the girl said. 'I want to get the number settled. Please say you'll come.'

'I really can't commit myself at the moment.' Ann spoke thoughtfully. She didn't want to hurt the girl's feelings, but she knew what would happen if she went to the party and Hugh was there, and she didn't want to ask outright if Hugh would be going. Petra would sense there was something amiss, and that might add further complications.

'Have you found yourself a man?' Petra demanded. 'If so, bring him along.'

'No, it's nothing like that, but you

know how it is here!' Ann felt justified in exaggerating a little.

'All right! I'll let you off the hook, but do try and come, Ann. There are some more old friends you'll be glad to meet again. John Goymer is back in town, and he's keen to see you again.'

'John!' Ann nodded to herself. 'Of course, I remember him! He went out to the Middle East; something to do with oil, wasn't it?'

'That's right! He'd like to see you again, Ann.'

'All right, let me just check with Mother and Father, and I'll call you back.' Ann suppressed a sigh. 'It's on Saturday evening, you said!'

'Yes. Any time around seven-thirty will do.' Petra sounded relieved.

'I'll make it then, but I shan't stay late. I have to be up at five on Sunday morning.'

'Five!' Petra spoke with a shudder in her voice. 'I'm usually just thinking of going to bed about that time.' She chuckled. 'I shall be looking forward to seeing you, Ann.'

'I shan't disappoint you,' Ann replied.

But she was thoughtful as she replaced the receiver, and her thoughts were with

Barry. She didn't like missing one evening when she could see him. Their duties failed to coincide sometimes, so there were evenings when they couldn't be together. She could have had an invitation for him, she knew, but she didn't want Hugh to know that she was interested in Barry.

She had arranged to see Barry that afternoon down by the brook, but rain was smearing down, although not too heavily, and after she had eaten her lunch, Ann began to prepare to go and meet the man she loved. There were butterflies inside her as she donned her raincoat, and her heart was leaping expectantly as she set out for the path.

The rain was coming down heavier than she had thought, but she kept going, knowing that Barry would be watching from the house to see her leaving. Then he would follow. She didn't look back although it was a great temptation to do so. Her feet slipped on the path, which was treacherous with fallen leaves, and she was glad she'd put on her thick shoes.

Ann had to stand under a tree because of the sudden downpour that descended, and she spotted Barry coming along the path, apparently following her footsteps. A smile touched her lips and she shook her head quickly to dash away the raindrops adhering to her face. He saw her and waved, and she felt a thrill go through her as she replied.

The sight of him never failed to send a shiver along her spine, and she drew a deep breath and held it for a moment while she considered him.

She was in love with him. The days following the revelation along this very path had done nothing to make her change her mind about that. In fact she was more convinced than ever that they had been meant for each other. At first she had been anxious about his feelings, but he seemed to be coming even closer towards her. She was not learning much about him! He didn't say much about himself, and he seemed so very quiet. He had no strong opinions about anything, and although she liked peace and quietness, she was able to hold forth quite strongly on certain subjects. But Barry seemed to be most placid, and she loved him for his gentleness and consideration.

When he came up with her he was breathless, and he took her into his arms and held her for long moments. She could feel that his face was wet, and she kissed him lovingly.

'I thought perhaps it would be raining too hard for you,' he remarked at length.

'I don't mind what the weather's like so long as you're with me,' she replied.

'That's how I feel about it.' He pulled back and looked at her keenly, smiling, his blue eyes dull because of the rain. 'I keep telling myself that this isn't really happening to me, Ann. I feel too happy to be able to accept it without misgiving. My feelings are that no one can be this happy. I haven't deserved it.'

'I've felt the same way,' she responded. 'But this is the height of perfection, Barry. We were meant for this, and that's why everything seems to fit just so. I have come back to England just to meet you.'

'Until you came into my life I thought I was doomed to bitter disappointment. I'm a sentimentalist, you know. I believe in romance and all things connected with it. I used to tell myself that somewhere in the world there was a girl who was made just for me, who would fit in with me and my way of life. But I never thought I would meet her. Now here you are, and I can hardly believe my luck.'

She smiled, getting a thrill from his words. He kissed her, and she was unmindful of the raindrops splashing into her face from the soaked branches overhead. She clung to him strongly, wanting more of the joy his lips gave to her.

'I love you, Barry,' she said softly, her eyes wide with adoration. 'Life seems to be worthwhile now. There's more to every day than just duty. When I think of you the time seems to go much faster, and I know that when I get off duty you'll be around somewhere, just waiting for me.'

'I'm always waiting for you,' he responded gently. 'My dearest girl.' He kissed her again and held her close.

They did not walk because of the rain, which seemed to isolate them in their own small world of love, and it was quite pleasant under the tree, holding each other close and watching the splashing rain sweeping across the fields.

'We find our pleasure in the simpler things,' Barry observed. 'That's a good sign, Ann!'

'I don't care where we are or what happens so long as we're together!' she replied.

168

He studied her damp face for some moments, and Ann kept her features expressionless. She loved to look into his eyes, and could see herself faintly in their pale depths.

'If anyone saw us here like this they would think we're mad,' he observed.

'I don't care! This is better than being inside. At least we are alone here.' She snuggled up against him, her eyes closing. He was leaning against the trunk of the tree, supporting her with his strong arms. 'Petra Grahame called me just before I came out,' she told him, and went on to explain about the coming party. 'I don't want to go. I'd rather spend the time with you, but Petra was most insistent.'

'Then you must go!' He tilted her face with gentle fingers under her chin and kissed her lightly. 'I shall be on duty Saturday, anyway. Your father asked me to stand in for him. He's got to go to York for the evening.'

'Well that eases the situation!' She nodded slowly. 'I didn't want to go because I thought I'd miss the chance of seeing you, but if you're going to be unavailable then I'll make the party. It will satisfy Petra, and she won't bother me so soon again.'

'You've got to get out and lead a full life,' Barry said. 'It won't do for you to tie yourself down to me to the exclusion of all others.'

'I want to be with you every opportunity I have,' she protested.

'That would suit me admirably, but you'll become narrow minded if you exclude everything else from your life. I shall always be on hand when you want to see me.'

'You don't believe that two people should spend as much time as possible together? We have only one life, you know, and we can spend it just once.'

'I agree with you, but it could be a mistake to bind yourself to me.'

She felt a bit daunted by his words, but did not show it. She didn't want to tie him down if that wasn't what he wanted, and she didn't regard it as being tied down, anyway! She felt a bit crest-fallen as she regarded his intent face, but she was careful not to let him see it.

'What are we going to do this evening?' she asked lightly.

'We could go into town if you wish, although there's nothing much to do there. The weather is getting a bit bad for walking across country. It's too far to go into York just for the evening.' He paused and looked down into her face. 'Am I beginning to sound like a pessimist?' he demanded.

'You sound as if you're depressed.' She regarded him intently for a moment. 'You don't have anything on your mind, do you?'

'Not at all! I'm sometimes not very good company, Ann. I don't know why! I dislike crowds intensely and like being by myself.' He paused again and shook his head. 'That was before you came along, of course. Now I'm only happy when I'm with you. But I like to get you away from everything and have you completely to myself. Am I being selfish?'

'I don't think so!' She smiled, her confidence bright once more. 'I feel that way about you.'

'That's why I think you should get away from me sometimes when you're off duty. I could make your life very dull.'

'That's impossible! There's never a dull moment with you.'

'You fell in love with me first, remember.' He seemed to be serious. 'Now you've got to get to know me, and you'll

171

need some diversions to lighten the way.'

She did not reply, not wanting to prolong the subject. She shivered a little as she glanced across the fields. Rain was still sweeping down, and she could hear the solid pattering of it. But she liked the rain and she felt her pulses throbbing as if in sympathy with the heavenly drumming.

Later they started back to the house, and Ann was feeling a little bit uncertain. Barry had seemed to descend into some kind of a mood, and she was aware of it as they walked briskly through the rain. He held her arm tightly, his fingers hurting at times. When she glanced into his face she found his expression closed against her, although he smiled. But he was silent, and Ann could not help feeling that there was something on his mind.

'Will you come and have tea with me?' she asked as they reached the back gate of the Home.

'We're supposed to part here and go in separately, aren't we?' he countered.

'Only if you want to.' She watched his face intently, and sensed that he was uneasy about something.

'I don't like acting this way,' he went on. 'It makes me feel that there's something

172

wrong, that we have to hide the fact we're going out together.'

'Not for any reason on my part,' she reminded him.

'Well why should we care what anyone may think?' he demanded. 'I don't have to make a report on my private life, do I?'

'You don't,' she agreed.

'Then let's go in together and I will have tea with you.'

Her eyes glinted with pleasure at his words and she clung to his arm as they went on. They were both fairly wet by the time they entered the Home, and Ann felt happier and more easy as they went into the private quarters she shared with her parents.

She was pleased that both her parents were not there, although they would be in to tea at any time. She took Barry's raincoat and hung it up to drip dry, and she gave him a towel to dry himself. She had barely begun to prepare tea for them when her mother arrived.

'Hello, Barry,' Mrs Bowman greeted, her dark eyes taking in the unmistakable signs about him. It was evident he had been out in the rain. 'Has Ann forced you into going out in such weather?'

'I don't mind the weather,' he replied.

Ann looked out from the small kitchen. 'Hello, Mother! What are you having for tea?'

'Just a snack until later. But don't let me interrupt your preparations for tea.' Mrs Bowman frowned as she took in Ann's flushed face and wet hair. 'You two must be quite mad to go out wandering in the rain.'

'If we took heed of the weather we'd never get out at this time of the year,' Ann retorted with a smile. She saw a questioning light in her mother's eyes, and smiled enigmatically. 'We walked along the footpath, and it was lovely in the rain.'

'We all have our pet likes, but I'm glad to say that walking in the rain isn't one of mine.' Mrs Bowman smiled as she nodded.

'Well I suppose it does depend on who you're with,' Ann said. She saw Barry glance at her, and she smiled. 'He's quite good company, you know. The time went so quickly.'

'I can see that you're wondering about this,' Barry said. He was smiling, but Ann had the feeling he was a bit self conscious. 'I broke my engagement. It wasn't going to

174

work out. So there can be no complications because I was out with Ann.'

Mrs Bowman nodded. She was smiling, and Ann was pleased her mother was so understanding.

'You haven't let that fact become generally known, have you?' she asked.

'I haven't, but I will if you think I ought to.' Barry was ready, almost eager to please.

'Perhaps that would be a good thing. You know someone will have seen you out together, and this isn't the first time, is it? I've seen you going off separately, but I was certain you were meeting somewhere.'

'I have been getting some curious glances from some of the staff,' Ann said. 'I hadn't given much thought to it until now. I expect that's the reason.'

'Then you'd better start letting it out that I'm no longer engaged,' Barry said. 'We have to think of your reputation.'

She nodded, filled with relief. She wanted everything above board. She wanted everyone to know that she and Barry were seeing one another. Her mother was watching her closely, but Ann did not care what was showing in her face.

'I'll see to it that everyone does know

within the next few days,' she said. 'Now if you'll excuse me I'll get back to preparing tea.'

She was happy as she went back into the kitchen, leaving her mother to talk to Barry. She was finding that the afternoon had produced mixed feelings inside her. Barry had seemed to slip into a mood for some unknown reason, and she tried to think back over what had been said. It could have been something she said! She knew he had spoken the truth when he said they'd fallen in love first, and now had to get to know one another. But she felt that she knew all she really needed to know about him. The rest they could pick up as they went along.

When they sat down to a meal, Mrs Bowman joined them, and the conversation around the table was animated. Frank Bowman appeared shortly for tea, and he was pleased to see Barry present.

'I was thinking only this afternoon that we ought to have you in here more often, Barry,' he said eagerly. 'I know Ann must be feeling a bit lonely after her time abroad. This is a quiet place, and dull, I suppose, for younger people.'

'I don't find it dull,' Ann said quickly.

176

'This is my home, and there have been many times in the past when I've wished I could have been here. You'll never find me complaining about Clover House. If I never move away again I'll be happy.'

'Well spoken!' Frank Bowman regarded Ann for a moment. 'Spoken like the dutiful child that you are. But I must tell you that I'm getting some reports about you, Ann. Sister Corbin is most pleased with the way you handle your duties.'

'I couldn't be any less than perfect, could I?' she demanded, her dark eyes glinting. 'If I did less than my best I'd have everyone saying that I was taking advantage of the fact that my parents run this place.'

'So you think we put you at a disadvantage, do you?' Mrs Bowman demanded.

'No. I'm not the kind of girl who can give less than her best. But it would have been awkward for me if I'd been the lazy type.'

'I've let Mr Oakley have some reading material,' Frank Bowman went on. 'He's worried me every single time I've visited him. I think the slight exertions that he'll put on himself by reading will outweigh the harm he's doing himself fretting at the enforced inactivity.'

'He's making good progress, wouldn't you say?' Barry asked.

'Certainly. We're beginning to have a good effect upon him, but he's still got a long way to go yet.'

Ann was relieved that the subject had got around to business, and she listened intently as they chatted on, talking first about one patient and then another. This was the sort of conversation she always remembered. It came up at every mealtime, without fail, and she understood it and could take part in it.

She watched Barry's face throughout the meal, noting his reactions and listening to everything he said with a careful consideration. She had to learn all there was to know about him; what made him tick and his likes and dislikes, and she realized that in her turn she was being studied by Barry. He smiled whenever their glances met, and she knew she could hardly wait to get alone with him again. She wanted to feel his arms about her, to experience the thrilling sensations that filled her when they kissed. Surely that was sufficient to carry them along through

178

life. The fact that she felt she could hardly live without him had to be enough basis for love, everlasting love.

When the meal was over both her parents returned to duty, and Barry helped her clear away. She washed the tea things and he wiped. He was silent, obviously lost in deep thoughts, and Ann watched him all the time, studying him critically, trying to find if there was anything about him she did not like. But he came through the analysis with flying colours.

'Well?' he demanded suddenly, when they had finished the chores. 'Have you come to any conclusions about me?' He smiled as he placed his hands upon her shoulders. 'You've been watching me like a hawk ever since we sat down to tea. What's in your mind now?'

'I was just thinking how much I love you,' she said softly, and his face became serious as he looked into her dark eyes.

'I love you, Ann, but I can't help thinking that perhaps you are deceiving yourself about me.'

'Why should you think that?' She frowned as she waited for his reply.

'You might have turned to me on the rebound, as it were, without realizing it,

179

that is. What you may think now is love may later turn out to be something much less.'

'No.' She shook her head slowly. 'I couldn't be more sure about this if I had known you a hundred years.'

He took her into his arms, and Ann clung to him, hoping in some way to communicate her feelings to him. She wanted him to understand that she loved him purely and simply. There were no attendant circumstances that had forced her into it. The emotion had come of its own free will, and she was well aware of it. But she wanted to rid him of his doubts.

'I don't doubt you, Ann,' he said softly. 'Never think that. But I want you to be sure for your own safety. If anything happened to convince you that I am not the right man after all, it would just about smash your life. So be pretty certain about your feelings before you commit yourself in any way.'

She nodded, unable to argue with the logic of his words. 'I will be certain of myself if I ever make a decision,' she promised.

'That's all I ask!' He kissed her gently, and Ann melted into his arms as if she had been his sweetheart for years.

But she could not help wondering what lay near the surface of his mind to bother him. It was evident that he was not concerned about himself. He seemed pretty sure of his own feelings. Yet he was afraid that she was blinding herself in some obscure way, that she might imagine herself to be in love with him when she was experiencing something much less.

Time seemed to be the only answer to that problem. It would take time to show him how much she felt for him. Perhaps that was why most couples waited before declaring their feelings. They had to make sure. Ann tried to find some patience, but she was strangely short of that quality. She felt a sudden urgency in wanting to make Barry aware that she was not suffering from a delusion in thinking she was in love with him. Nothing else mattered in the whole wide world.

Chapter Nine

Saturday arrived with nothing changing Ann's mind about going to Petra's party. She was reluctant to go because she knew she would meet Hugh Leighton there. But then she needed to talk to Hugh personally to put him straight about his intentions towards her. She knew that no amount of refusing him over the telephone would convince him that she had no interest in him. So she prepared for the party, and looked forward to seeing Barry before departing.

Her parents went off during the afternoon and did not expect to return until early hours of the next morning. Barry was on duty; merely on call should an emergency arise, and Ann spent some time during the afternoon with him.

'I'm still not keen on going to this party this evening,' she told him. They were in the sitting room with the television on. Barry was watching sport, and Ann was interested only in his presence.

'If you don't go you'll be here all alone,' he retorted. 'I shall be in the duty office working on reports and charts. I shan't be able to be with you until much later, Ann.'

'Oh, I'll go, but it isn't something I wish to make a habit of.'

'That's right. Go and enjoy yourself. You stick it out here day after day. I never seem to take you anywhere pleasant. When we're off duty we either sit in here or walk the footpaths.'

'It isn't your fault that the weather is against us,' she retorted strongly.

He chuckled. 'I'm teasing you now. I seem to have got into the habit of belittling my attempts to show you around and have a good time. I expect I am a stick in the mud of sorts if you compare me with some of the other men you've known.'

'What's that got to do with it?' she countered. 'I fell in love with you the way you are, not in the hope that I'll change you later. Why do you look down upon yourself, Barry?'

'I don't go that far, do I?' He smiled slowly and shook his head. 'I shall have to be careful or I'll give you the wrong impression of myself.'

'You couldn't do that. I know all I need to about you, and not a thing can you do to make me change my beliefs.'

'Stick to your guns.' He smiled as he took her into his arms. 'I'm not trying to make you think deeply about this thing that's between us. I think I'm trying to convince myself that it is really happening. So don't pay too much heed to what I say or think.'

'I don't,' she retorted lightly, and he shook his head as he regarded her.

'You're the most beautiful girl in the world,' he said flatly.

She smiled, watching his face. There was an intent expression on his features which she had come to like. His eyes seemed to glint with unholy pleasure. She sensed there was something of a devil in him trying to get out, and she wished he would let go of himself sometimes, forget his responsibilities and have a really good time. But he was serious minded, and she knew she would have to adapt herself to his way of life. There might have to be sacrifices made, but true love was a worthwhile goal, and she didn't care what it might cost her.

They had tea together, and then Barry had to go on duty. He departed, advising her to have a good time at the party, and she sat thinking for quite some time after he'd left her. She didn't want to try and enjoy herself without him. It would be an empty pleasure without his company. That was the extent of her involvement with him.

When she was ready to go out she checked her reflection in a full length mirror and then departed, leaving by the back door to go to the garages. She drove her mother's Fiat and was soon speeding towards town. Rain spattered against the windscreen, and she set the wipers working. Her mind worked fast as she mused upon the whole intangible situation that seemed to grip her.

But her mind was clear of worry. There were no problems in her life. She had left all the clouds behind before coming home, and she felt satisfied that she'd managed to conclude that phase of her life satisfactorily.

There was a small knot of nervousness inside her when she rang the bell at Petra's flat. She was later than she had been expected to arrive, and heard the sounds of revelry in the flat when Petra opened the door.

'Ann! I'd almost given you up for lost! Come in and make yourself at home.' Petra was radiant, and Ann was surprised at her friend's elation. 'I'm so glad you came. I wanted to see you to talk rather seriously to you, and yet the party isn't the best place for chatting. However we can make plans to talk some other time. This evening you must enjoy yourself with the rest of us.'

'You know I shan't be able to stay long, don't you?' Ann said cautiously.

'Yes. You did mention something about having to be up at five in the morning!' Petra pulled a face and shook her head. 'What on earth induced you to become a nurse? Getting up at that time in the morning would be a miracle for me. In fact I don't think it could ever be arranged. But let me take your coat and I'll take you into the big room. There are one or two people I want you to meet.'

Ann felt relieved when she looked around the large room into which Petra ushered her and failed to spot Hugh Leighton. Hugh had been in the back of her mind ever since she'd reluctantly accepted the invitation. But he wasn't here!

There were others she knew, and soon she was in the midst of a group of old friends who were eager to hear of her adventures abroad. Ann talked freely, enjoying herself, and she didn't realize that time was slipping by so quickly until Petra came to her side.

'I can guess that very soon now you're going to look me up to say goodnight,' Petra said. 'I won't try to detain you longer than you want to stay, Ann. But I would like to have a chat with you.'

'Well that can easily be arranged.' Ann was feeling in an expansive mood. She'd been plied with drinks, although she had refused a great many, and she felt warm and cosy inside, held up by the knowledge that Barry was there at the nursing home and that they were in love. She glanced at her watch and knew she ought to be leaving, and she looked into Petra's eyes and saw that the girl was pleased with her.

'Can I come and see you tomorrow?' Petra asked.

'I shall be off duty from two onwards.'

'But will you have anything else to do?'

'I expect I shall be going out later on, but you can come and see me if you wish. I'll look out for you, shall I?'

'About three?' Petra asked.

'That will do fine. But what's the trouble? You sound as if you've put your foot into it somehow. What can I do to help?'

'There's a doctor at the nursing home!'

'Barry Lander!' Ann felt a pang go through her. 'What do you know about him?'

'Nothing personally, but he's just broken off his engagement with Olive Ferber.'

'I don't think I know her.'

'You wouldn't. She's not a local girl. But I know her well. She's a good customer of mine, and when I saw her yesterday she was really upset.'

'Because the engagement has been broken off?' Ann blinked, but she kept her face expressionless.

'Yes. She thinks the world of Doctor Lander. But he's not in love with her, apparently.'

'Then what do you want me to do, Petra?' Ann was frowning now. 'Surely you don't expect me to intercede on your friend's behalf!'

'No!' Petra shook her head. 'That wouldn't work, would it? And if he didn't love Olive then she wouldn't be happy with him even if he married her.' The girl smiled slowly. 'I'm interested in him myself, after listening to Olive. I was hoping you could introduce me to him.'

'And that's why you want to come out to the nursing home?' Ann smiled. 'I couldn't help you there, Petra. Doctor Lander will probably be on duty, anyway.'

'I know he doesn't get much free time, but I would like to see him if at all possible. You're my friend, Ann, and your parents own the Home. Surely you can do a little thing like that for me. Why not ask me to tea tomorrow evening, and have him present as well?'

'You don't want much, do you?' Ann smiled. 'But I think it could be arranged.' She was wondering what Barry would do with an eager woman chasing him. But she didn't want to start something that might get out of hand! The thought crossed her mind and held her for a moment.

'Shall I come tomorrow then?' Petra demanded anxiously.

'Certainly, although I can't promise to have Doctor Lander to tea. If he's on duty then he won't be available.'

'Don't you like him, Ann?' the girl asked. 'I envy you and your work, you know. But I was never cut out to be anything important in life.'

'I like him. He seems to be a very nice person. But you'd find him quiet, Petra. He's not your type at all.'

'And what is my type?' Petra demanded.

'You like plenty of fun and late hours. Doctor Lander thinks only of his duty, and when he's off duty nothing suits him better than to get out with his easel and canvas to do some painting.'

'He's artistic!' Petra's eyes gleamed. 'Has he painted any local scenes?'

'I think so. I saw him doing one just after I arrived home.'

'I might be able to sell them for him. I've got several outlets for that sort of thing. Oh, I must talk to him.'

'Very well. Come to the Home at three tomorrow afternoon and I'll see what I can do for you. I'll ask Doctor Lander to tea, and you'll get the chance to talk to him.' Ann thought for a moment, and she pictured Barry's face. 'But I don't think you'd better mention to him that you know his ex-fiancée. It might be a sore point with him at the moment. I'll introduce you as my friend. In fact he knows I'm here at your party this evening.'

'So you're on friendly terms with him!'

'Of course! I come into contact with him every day. Why should I not be on friendly terms with him?'

'I wish I could step into your shoes for a day!' Petra sighed heavily.

'You sound as if you're in love with him already, and yet you haven't even met him!'

'I've seen a photograph of him. He seems to be the kind of man who could fill my life.'

'You're twenty-four, Petra, not a teen-ager,' Ann said, and although she smiled she could not prevent a pang striking through her breast.

'That's what's on my mind! I'm twenty-four. It's about time I settled down, isn't it?'

'You know a great many eligible young men.'

'And all of them bore me. They're men like Hugh!'

'Where is he tonight? Why isn't he at the party?'

'He's got something else on his mind.'

'I thought he was going to start pestering me! He's been ringing me every day at the Home.' Ann shook her head slowly. 'I heard he's practically engaged to a girl who lives in York.'

'So I've heard! But you know Hugh! He's not the marrying kind. But I'll bring him to tea tomorrow night if you like!'

'No thanks!' Ann shook her head. 'Hugh isn't my kind of man.'

'But Doctor Lander is mine!' Petra smiled as she looked into Ann's dark eyes.

'I do believe you only asked me here tonight because you wanted to get at Barry Lander!'

'Well one good turn does deserve another! I'll see you at three tomorrow afternoon, shall I?'

'Yes. I'd better be going now, anyway. Thanks for the fun, Petra.'

'I'll see you off the premises,' the girl replied, smiling.

Ann was thoughtful as she drove herself home. She had the feeling that she was doing the wrong thing in bringing Petra into contact with Barry, but she was also aware that if Petra had set her mind to meeting Barry then it would be better to arrange that meeting and act in a supervisory capacity. She felt that Barry would soon discourage the girl, and that would be that. But Petra had to try her hand, and the sooner it was done the better!

It was a clear night, and Ann soon reached the Home. She put away the car and walked to the rear of the house, entering quietly and making her way to the private wing. She hadn't really enjoyed her evening, but that was not the fault of the party. If Barry had been with her it would have been so different, but she was glad she hadn't arranged for him to accompany her, and when she went to bed she was already dreading the morrow ...

Just after five she was awake and getting ready for duty. She nibbled breakfast, and reported for duty at six. Sister Corbin was on duty when she entered the office, and the woman smiled a cheerful good morning. Ann was still feeling sleepy, but she made an effort to become efficient and she went about the routine work with no sign on her that she was worried.

The morning advanced and the Home slowly assumed its normal atmosphere. Visitors were allowed in the morning as well as afternoon and evening, and at ten, as the first visitors arrived, Ann went off duty for a thirty-minute break. As she walked along the corridor to her quarters she saw Barry approaching.

'Hello!' His face eased from a firm expression when he saw Ann. 'Did you have a nice time last night. I thought about you a great deal.'

'It was all right as far as parties go, but I would rather have been out with you, Barry,' she replied. She was thinking of Petra, and wondered what kind of an impression the girl would make on him. 'Will you come to tea this evening?'

'Certainly. I'm off duty, and I think we should get together.'

'I don't know if you'll agree with what I've done!' She paused as she considered just how much she should tell him about Petra. It had been a debatable point all morning. Should she tell him all about Petra or throw him in at the deep end with the girl? She sighed and she tried to make up her mind, but even now she could not bring herself to give him the full facts.

'What have you done?' he demanded, watching her closely, and Ann dragged herself from her thoughts and moistened her lips.

'I've asked Petra to tea this evening. I'd like you to meet her. She's been my friend ever since we were at school, and I missed her a great deal when we were apart.'

'I'd like to meet her!' He nodded. 'I shall be looking forward to this afternoon. But we shan't be able to get out by ourselves after tea, shall we?'

'I expect Petra will stay on through the evening,' she replied slowly.

'I'll see you after you get off duty, shall I? I've got to make my round now.'

'Petra will be here about three!'

'That's not so good. I shan't have you much to myself today, shall I?'

'I'm sorry, Barry, but I thought I'd better get Petra here and get it over with.'

'That's all right. Any friend of yours is a friend of mine.' He smiled and went on, and Ann sighed again as she walked on. She fancied that Petra would have the same idea about Barry when they met.

After her break she went back on duty, but Barry had finished his round, and disappeared again. She reported to Sister Corbin, who went off on her break, and when she sat down at the desk to keep an eye on the twenty or so patients on the ground floor the indicator board began buzzing.

Her first call was to Mr Oakley's room, and Ann found him staring disconsolately from the window when she entered his room. He looked round at her, and nodded briefly.

'Hi, Nurse! It's nice to see you. Can you get me a newspaper to read? I've gone through the books your father let me have, and I'm just itching to get hold of a newspaper.'

'I'll see if I can get you one,' she retorted. 'But don't let on that you got it from me if you're caught with it. You know you're not permitted to read the news in case there's anything that might upset you!'

'Sure, I know. Now it wouldn't be a bad idea if you had a nice friend you could get to visit me here. I don't get to talk to anyone except the staff, and their one topic is my physical condition.'

Ann stared at him as an idea took root in her mind. Petra! She smiled. 'As a matter of fact I do have a friend who might come and visit you. She asked me enough questions about what life was like abroad, and if you tell her about the States then you'll interest her.' She paused. 'Are you married, Mr Oakley?'

'No!' He shook his head. 'I've been all kinds of fool in my time, but never that. Of course, I'm beginning to think that I made a mistake. Now I'm getting a bit long in the tooth there's no one to take care of me. But bring along your friend and I promise to keep her entertained.'

'She's coming to have tea with me today. I'll bring her here if you like.'

'I'd like it very much.' A smile came to his face. 'My parents are coming over to see me as soon as my father can get time off from his job. But he's a key man and they can't do without him. I sure could do with a smiling face around here and a fresh mind that don't have my welfare plastered all over it.'

Ann smiled. 'I'll bring Petra along this afternoon,' she promised.

'Petra!' He looked startled for a moment. 'That is one strange name. Your friend ain't a dog by any chance, is she?'

'No, Petra is short for Petrina. She's a very nice girl. She's my age and she can talk your ears off. You'd like her.'

198

'Just so I get the chance to talk to her,' he said, smiling. 'Thanks for the effort, Nurse.'

'I'll have to run along now,' Ann said. 'Sister is away on her break and I've got the floor to myself. I expect the indicator board is jangling itself to pieces.'

She slipped out of the room and hurried back to the office, and several indicators were buzzing. She shook her head and started making a round, hurrying to answer the calls, never knowing if one could be an emergency or not. But she found no trouble, and eventually caught up with her work.

When she had some moments to spare she considered what she had done. If she could get Petra interested in Mr Oakley then so much the better. It would take the pressure off herself for one thing, and give Mr Oakley something to look forward to. Petra was a good hearted girl, and she might enter into the spirit of the thing.

Sister Corbin returned, and Ann was pleased that the morning was passing. But she had only just left the office when the telephone rang, and Sister Corbin came to the door and called to her.

'It's a call for you, Ann!'

'Oh!' Ann frowned as she returned and took the receiver. Sister Corbin left the office, and Ann gave her name.

'Guess who!' a man's voice said loudly.

'Hugh!' Ann compressed her lips. 'I've asked you not to call me when I'm on duty!'

'This is different, it's Sunday,' he retorted.

'It may be different to you, but it's the same as any day in this place.' She glanced at her watch. The time was just after eleven. 'I suppose you've just got up!'

'Of course! That's what Sunday mornings are for! Everyone lies in on Sunday!' He stifled a yawn loudly.

'I was up at five,' she said firmly.

'Poor old you! But I could put a stop to all that, you know!'

'Really! That's a surprising offer! Exactly what do you have in mind?'

'Marry me!'

She made no reply, and she could hear him chuckling at the other end of the line. She waited until his merriment had ceased.

'You sound in very high spirits this morning. Where were you last night? Didn't you get an invitation to Petra's party?'

'I did, and even though I knew you'd be there I just couldn't make it.'

'Then your other business must have been important!' She chuckled. 'I expect you were in York making arrangements for your wedding!'

'That'll be the day!' He sounded grim. 'There's been only one girl in my life, and that's for as long as I can remember. I thought I'd lost her once, when she went off to marry another fellow. But now she's back and I'm not going to let anything or anyone put me off this time.'

'Do I know this girl?' Ann demanded, although she could guess what was coming.

'You know her very well! I'm talking to her now! She's the most beautiful and generous girl I've ever met, and I know she's meant for me. I love you, Ann, and I want to see you to tell you to your face. We've been apart far too long, and we've got to do something about this. I'm very much in love with you and I want you to know it. I'll come round this afternoon and see you. I must talk to you.'

'No, Hugh,' she said firmly, her senses reeling as she tried to prevent her mind becoming confused. 'I'm afraid I shan't be here this afternoon!' She could think of no other excuse in the heat of the moment.

'Petra is coming to tea with you this afternoon,' he retorted. 'Don't try to put me off, Ann, because it won't work. You are my girl in future, and no one will ever be able to deny it. I'll bring Petra out to the Home this afternoon at three, and we'll carry on from there.'

Before Ann could deny him or say anything the line went dead, and she stood looking at the receiver as if she had lost her powers of reasoning. There was a big blank in her mind while she tried to fight down her panic, and she could see nothing but complications ahead.

Chapter Ten

The rest of that Sunday morning was like a nightmare to Ann. She found it difficult to concentrate upon her duties, and time passed her by without impressing upon her its flight or progress. She worked hard, maintaining an expressionless face when confronted by any of the staff, but she was like ice inside, and her mind was struggling to break through the shock which filled her.

First Petra was forcing herself into the situation, and the girl plainly had every intention of making herself attractive to Barry. Now Hugh was coming, intent upon forcing the issues for his own selfish reasons, and Ann began to wonder if some sort of a conspiracy existed between Hugh and Petra. Had Hugh enlisted Petra's aid in this attempt to make Ann his wife? Had Hugh found out in some way that she was in love with Barry? Or at least discovered that she and Barry were walking out together!

She did not know what to believe, but she could not accept the situation, and by the time she was relieved from duty her brain was afire with nagging questions and her mind chafed because she could not find suitable answers.

But the afternoon and evening would certainly make matters clear, and she determined, as she went to the private wing to get out of her uniform, that she would stand no nonsense from Hugh and wouldn't permit Petra to gain any initiative with Barry.

She was limp and tired as she stripped off her uniform and went into the bathroom to take a most welcome shower. She ran the water until it was comfortably hot, then stood under the streaming jets and closed her eyes, feeling the thrumming water driving the tiredness out of her system. She was reluctant to emerge from the haven of water, but time was remorseless now, and she hurriedly dried herself and then went to dress.

She selected a green dress with black piping and three-quarter sleeves, pinning a golden lover's-knot brooch at the throat. Her black hair shone as she brushed it and set it in the style that most suited her. When she was ready she studied her reflection in the mirror, and tried to force the worry from her dark eyes. There were a few moments only left before she expected Petra and Hugh to arrive, and she tried desperately to compose herself.

Ann was still trying to decide whether or not to tell Barry something of the situation that confronted them. If he knew Petra was going to set her cap at him then he might be better able to withstand any temptation which might come his way. But she felt that if he knew what was going on he might become interested in Petra even against his will, and then he would be lost.

She realized her attitude was naturally selfish, and she felt a pang of jealousy, unaccustomed but severely painful. She paced the long sitting room as she awaited the fateful hour, and when the minutes slipped by after the hour and there was no sign of Petra and Hugh she began to hope against hope that they were not coming.

Then Hugh arrived, and she started nervously at the knock on the sitting room door. She opened it quickly, her eyes gleaming and her lips parted, for she expected it to be Barry, but Hugh stood there, firm and determined. He took a deep breath as he looked at her, and she saw admiration fill his eyes.

'Ann, I have never seen you looking lovelier,' he said softly.

'Come in, Hugh!' She moved out of the doorway and permitted him to enter. 'Look, I don't want to sound stuffy, but I wish you wouldn't talk like that, especially in front of Petra and Doctor Lander.' She paused, frowning. 'Where is Petra? You said you were bringing her!'

'We met Doctor Lander down in the hall, and Petra clung to him immediately. He's showing her around the Home, and they'll come on up here later. But why can't I talk about the way I feel for you? I'm not ashamed of my love!'

'You've shocked me by what you said over the telephone,' she admitted. 'We've been friends for a very long time, Hugh, but we have never shown any interest in one another. I'm not in love with you and I don't think I could ever be so. We were meant to be friends and that's all.'

'Well I'm not going to accept that. There's no one else in your life. You've just got back from abroad and you left Gerry over there. I let you get away from me before, and I'm not going to permit that to happen again.'

She sighed heavily. 'I don't want any trouble with you, Hugh, but I must make it plain that I can never love you. Can you understand that?'

'I can understand what you're saying, but I don't understand why. I love you, Ann. It's taken me too long to get around to telling you, but now that I've broken the ice I shall tell you every day.'

Ann sighed heavily. She began to feel that she had been trapped into this situation, and there seemed no way out without trouble. What would Barry think if he came upon them while Hugh was professing love for her in his very loud tones? Then she thought of Petra, and could imagine the girl crowding Barry, trying to impress him and get him interested in herself. She wished now that she hadn't seen Petra on her return home.

'Ann! Surely you can see how serious I am!' Hugh was closing upon her now, determined to press his suit to the limit. 'I wouldn't come here making a fool of myself if I wasn't deadly serious. I can't sleep at nights, thinking of you. I didn't realize just how much I do love you until it hit me when I saw you were home. But even when you were away I used to wonder about you and tell myself that I missed you.'

'Hugh, there's no room in my life for you,' she said fiercely. 'Can't you understand? You're embarrassing me with your insistence. I have no wish to hurt you or cause you any pain or unhappiness, but you're heading for trouble if you press this.'

'There's nothing else I can do,' he replied, shaking his head, following her across the room. 'I can't control my feelings any longer. If I didn't come here today to tell you about them I would have burst like a balloon. There's no one else in your life, so why are you so certain you can't love me?'

'We've known each other for so long,' she said. 'If we were meant to fall in love it would have happened years ago. Now please desist, Hugh. You're greatly complicating matters.'

'So my love means nothing to you!' His brown eyes were hard, narrowed and bitter.

'I could never love you, and I would be doing you great harm by giving you any encouragement! Can't you see? You've told me of your feelings and I can't reciprocate them. I'm sorry, but the longer you press me the worse it's going to be for the both of us.'

'How can I get through to you?' he demanded heavily.

'You can't!' She shook her head impatiently.

'But you can't deny me the chance to catch you! Every man is entitled to try and win the girl he loves.'

Ann was beginning to get worried. She didn't want Barry to come upon this scene. Hugh was worked up now, his face showing his deeper feelings, and he wouldn't care who saw or heard him.

'There is someone else!' he said strongly. 'I can sense it. Tell me, Ann!'

'There is,' she said slowly.

His face slowly lost all expression. His eyes narrowed and grew hostile, and Ann watched him with a kind of frightened fascination. She hadn't thought a human face could summon up such emotion. Then he sighed bitterly and let his shoulders sag.

'So that's it! But it isn't possible! You haven't been home long enough to meet anyone. You're not the kind of girl to let anyone sweep you off your feet!'

'Well it happened this time,' she admitted.

'Who is it?'

She shook her head. 'I'd rather not say right now. He doesn't know about it himself, not yet.'

'Ah! Then it hasn't gone too far!'

'Far enough for me to realize that there could never be any other man for me.'

'Oh, Ann! If you'd only give me the chance to prove to you how much I love you!'

'It wouldn't help, Hugh. I would have to be in love with you before it could work, and I can never love you. I know that deep down inside, and that's what makes this whole thing so impossible.'

'All right!' He nodded slowly, his face like granite. 'I'll accept that. But we can still be friends, can't we?'

'Certainly, but that won't work after what you've told me here. It will always be between us, and you know it.' She was sad as she watched him. She certainly didn't want to hurt him, but she knew the truth was the only way, and if he was hurt now it wouldn't be as bad as the pain he might know later, if he was permitted to fool himself in the beginning.

'You want me to go away here now and never see you again?' His face was bleak as he spoke.

'Don't you think that would be the wisest thing?'

He shook his head and started to pace the room, and now his assurance was gone and his eyes proclaimed the hurt he was suffering. He paused to light himself a cigarette, and Ann noticed his fingers trembling.

'I'd set my mind on you the moment I knew you were back,' he said. 'You can't do this to me, Ann. Not twice. I suffered when it was known you were going away with Gerry. It was a nightmare I never really got over. Now this! Lightning doesn't strike twice in the same place!'

'It hurts me to see you suffering,' she said gently. 'But this is the easiest way in the long run. You'll get over it, Hugh!'

'Sure! I can get over a broken leg!' He smiled thinly. 'But it takes time, and what do I do in the meantime?'

She made no reply, and her happiness had faded sharply. She watched his intent face and could sense the anguish that gripped him, but there was nothing she could do for him, and she knew it. If he could only realize it too then he would make the necessary adjustments that much sooner and easier.

He watched her for long moments, trying to read her mind, and when she said nothing and gave no sign of relenting he sighed heavily and shook his head.

'I think I'd better go,' he said slowly. 'I wouldn't be good company after this, and I don't want to cause a scene. I'm sorry I pushed my way in here now, Ann. Please forgive me, won't you?'

'There's nothing to forgive,' she said slowly. 'I'm very sorry, Hugh.'

He smiled and turned away, walking swiftly to the door. He paused in the doorway and looked back at her, a brooding hopelessness in his dark eyes.

'I can find my own way out, Ann,' he said. 'See you around sometime!'

Before she could reply he was gone, and she heard his footsteps echoing in the corridor. She took a deep breath, held it for a moment, then released it slowly, and her senses seemed to dull and flag.

She went into the kitchen to do something about tea. She wanted to have everything ready for when tea time came. She didn't feel like leaving Petra alone with Barry. The prospect of spending the rest of the day with Petra making eyes at Barry didn't appeal to her, but she had to act the hostess no matter her feelings, and she forced herself to go on as if Hugh hadn't come and gone.

By the time she had finished preparing the meal she was wondering where Petra and Barry had got to, and she felt a pang of premonition seeping into her mind. She paced the room much as Hugh had done before leaving, and then she stood by the window and looked down over the gardens spread below.

There were clouds in the sky and they threatened rain. Wind rattled the panes, and leaves were falling from the trees, agitated and lost. Ann sighed heavily as she considered. She thought Hugh had spoiled the day, and Petra seemed intent upon doing what damage she could to Ann's own future, albeit unknowingly.

She was about to move from the window when she spotted movement on the far side of the gardens. She paused and narrowed her eyes, and a pang stabbed through her when she saw Barry and Petra together, walking slowly along one of the paths. Ann turned cold as she watched through narrowed brown eyes. She saw Petra look up into Barry's face, and the girl was smiling lightly, wearing the kind of expression she usually showed when flirting with a handsome man.

Ann moved back from the window and stayed watching. She saw Petra looking around, as if afraid of being disturbed. Barry seemed light hearted, and there was a smile on his face. He bent his head towards Petra, evidently asking the girl to repeat something which she said. Petra laughed and shook her head, and Ann was suddenly sickened by the whole thing.

Hugh had started the process inside her. He had put her joy to flight, and the fact that he was suffering because of his love for her added to the burden which seemed to attach itself to her mind. She felt a tinge of jealousy attack her attitude, and she fought vainly to overcome it. Jealousy was the last thing she wanted in her mind. She toyed with the idea of going down to the garden to interrupt them, but she knew she couldn't do that.

The afternoon had almost slipped away

before Ann heard footsteps in the corridor, and she tried to compose herself as she looked towards the door. There was a tap on the centre panel, and then the door was opened. She saw Barry and Petra standing there together, and the girl was smiling, her eyes alive with joyful animation.

'Ann!' The girl came into the room and hurried to Ann's side. 'I hope you won't feel neglected, but when I met Doctor Lander outside I just had to accept his invitation to look around. But I'm sure you see enough of the Home when you're on duty, don't you?'

'Hello, Petra. I was afraid you'd taken a dislike to Clover House and had departed.' Ann smiled cheerfully, but her eyes went to Barry's face. He seemed well pleased with himself and after he had closed the door he stood in the background, watching them. Ann tried to keep her expression neutral and her attitude friendly.

'No fear of that!' Petra was excelling herself, and Ann knew the girl had put on an act for Barry's sake and was now maintaining it. 'I'm half convinced that I ought to try and do something really worthwhile in my life.'

'Such as?' Barry demanded lightly, and

215

Ann did not miss the amused glance which Petra bestowed upon him.

'I might become a nurse.'

'You've left it a bit late in life to start training,' Ann said forcing a smile. 'But all candidates are welcomed.'

'Could I start here as a student nurse?'

'Are you serious?' Barry demanded.

'I think I am!' Petra nodded emphatically.

Ann smiled. She could just imagine Petra in a uniform, and getting up at five each morning, or working on night duty. But she said nothing, and the girl continued in her cheery strain. It was all Ann could do to contain her feelings. Petra was flirting outrageously with Barry, and he seemed to like the attentions the girl gave him.

'Where's Hugh?' Petra suddenly demanded. She had only just missed him. 'Don't tell me he's chasing the nurses already!'

'He had to leave,' Ann said. 'A telephone call! He said something about some unexpected business!'

Barry nodded, and his eyes held Ann's gaze for a moment. Ann wondered at the strange expression on his face, and suddenly wondered if Petra had been telling him about Hugh's love for her. If Petra suspected there might be something brewing between them then she would do all within her power to scotch it.

'That's a pity,' Petra said. 'Now I shall have to walk home. I wish Hugh would keep his business and his pleasures apart.'

'We'll drive you home later,' Barry said instantly, smiling at Ann.

'Certainly,' Ann said. 'But come and sit down, Petra. You must be cold. You didn't come dressed for rambling around the garden, did you?'

'Not really, but I don't get enough exercise and fresh air. I must try and discipline myself a little and make the effort to keep really fit. What do you suggest, Doctor?'

'You look pretty fit to me,' Barry said, smiling.

'Now you're flattering me,' she said, smiling prettily.

'You're on the go quite a lot, Petra,' Ann said. 'I expect you're fit.'

'Well you must be. I suppose nurses know everything about keeping fit.'

They sat down and began chatting

generally, and Ann found her friend's manner grating on her nerves. She could see Petra actually trying to attract Barry, and was faintly surprised that he didn't seem to notice anything out of the ordinary.

Petra kept trying to turn the conversation on to herself, and whenever Ann attempted to divert them the girl broached the subject of Hugh.

'You know, Ann, Hugh thinks the world of you,' the girl said on one occasion.

'Nonsense,' Ann scoffed, glancing at Barry. 'Hugh couldn't care less about any girl. He's too full of himself. He's not the marrying kind and never will be.'

'He's that way because he's so crazy about you! He was really upset when you went abroad.'

'I'd rather not talk about that,' Ann said rather sharply. She got to her feet. 'If you'll excuse me I'll get tea ready. I don't know if my parents will be joining us. I'd better check with Mother. Father is standing by this evening.'

'I'll come and help you, Ann,' Barry said, getting to his feet.

'I think you'd better stay here and keep Petra company,' Ann replied.

She was relieved to escape into the kitchen, and for a moment she stood with her hands to her face, her mind whirling with conjecture. She was confused by her reactions to the situation about her. Hugh had aroused her deepest sympathies, and Petra had loosed the worst of her emotions, making her feel completely out of her normal depth. She hoped Barry hadn't seen anything strange in her manner. But she had felt like telling Petra to stop her flirting on more than one occasion, and the knowledge that they still had to get through tea together almost unnerved her.

She was startled when the kitchen door opened at her back, and when she glanced over her shoulder she saw her mother standing there.

'I was coming to see if you and Father would be in to tea,' Ann said quickly.

'Yes, dear! I'll give you a hand. I've just looked in on Petra and Barry. They seem to have made friends quickly.'

'Petra is a friendly girl,' Ann retorted, and her tones sounded just a little too harsh in her own ears.

'Barry is able to make anyone feel at ease. It's a good quality about him. But I thought you said Hugh was coming!' Mrs

Bowman gave Ann a sharp glance.

'He did come, but he couldn't stay.' Ann did not meet her mother's eyes.

'I always liked Hugh! He's very pleasant. Did he come to see you specially, or just came along with Petra?'

'He brought Petra.'

'Was he at Petra's party last night?'

'No. He didn't say where he was, but he intimated that he couldn't get away from business.'

'What do you think of Hugh? Mrs Bowman let her words come easily, without emphasis. She came forward to help Ann open some cans of fruit.

'Hugh?' Ann suppressed a sigh. 'He and I were always good friends. I like him, and I value his friendship.'

'He likes you a lot, doesn't he?'

'He always did, I believe.'

'So you're going to find life complicated in future.'

'I don't think so. I rather fancy everything is clear cut.'

They worked in silence for some moments, and then Ann opened the kitchen door and prepared to transfer the dishes of fruit and the crockery into the dining room. She was relieved as she worked.

When the table was set she steeled herself to enter the sitting room to announce that tea was ready. As she opened the door she had a strange feeling that she ought to knock first, but when she looked into the room she found Barry and Petra seated apart, and Petra was talking animatedly. Ann paused in the doorway until the girl fell silent, and they both looked round at her.

'You've been a long time,' Barry commented. 'You should have let me help you.'

'Mother gave me a hand. But tea is ready now.'

Petra sprang to her feet, and she hastened to Ann's side, smiling vivaciously.

'This is a wonderful afternoon, Ann,' the girl said. 'I usually have such a dull time at the weekends.'

'I can't say the same about myself,' Ann retorted smiling.

They went into the dining room and Ann found her father present, helping her mother with the final preparations. Frank Bowman smiled as he shook hands with Petra.

'It's been a long time since I saw you, Petra,' he said.

'Not since before Ann went away,' the girl replied brightly.

'That's over three years, and yet it doesn't seem as if half that time has passed.' There was a note of regret in Frank Bowman's tones.

They sat down at the table, and Barry sat between Ann and Petra. Ann had been dreading the meal ever since Petra arrived, but it passed off without incident. Petra monopolized the conversation, and she kept addressing herself to Barry. It was all too obvious to Ann, but she made no comment, and she hoped that no one else noticed Petra's behaviour.

'This has been a marvellous time,' Petra said as the meal ended. 'I shall have to find an excuse for coming here more often.'

'You don't need an excuse to come,' Mrs Bowman said, smiling. 'You're always welcome, Petra. I can remember having you here to tea when you and Ann were schoolgirls. It doesn't seem possible that you've both grown up so well.'

'If you need an excuse to come here, I can give you one,' Ann said, and she was aware that Barry glanced quickly at her. Petra looked at her, nodding enthusiastically. 'We have a patient, an

American,' Ann went on. 'He's unmarried and has no visitors. His parents are trying to get over to see him, but he does need someone to talk to now and again, and I said I'd ask you to visit him once in a while. What do you think, Petra?'

'Well!' the girl was hesitant, and she glanced at Barry.

'It would help his condition,' Barry said instantly. 'I've been wondering about that same problem myself, Ann!'

'If it would help him then certain I'll visit him.' Petra spoke warmly, but her eyes showed Ann that she was not pleased with the suggestion. 'But how do I get out from town?'

'One of us will pick you up whenever you want to come in,' Frank Bowman said.

'And take you back to town afterwards,' Barry added.

'That sounds like a good arrangement.' Petra nodded. 'All right, I'll visit him. Do I meet him today?'

'I'll take you down and introduce you to him now we've had tea,' Ann said, before her father or Barry could offer. 'He has a heart condition, and mustn't exert himself at all, but you'll find him most interesting to talk to.'

'We'll clear the table and do the chores while you're away,' Mrs Bowman said. 'It's kind of you to do this, Petra.'

'Anything to help,' the girl said, and she cast a glance at Barry, as if seeking approval for her sacrifice.

Ann hoped she had caused a diversion sufficient to put Petra off her plans to get to know Barry. She was aware that the girl was not pleased with the situation, and Petra didn't speak as they went out from the private wing to the ground floor. But Ann was not certain now if this was the right course of action. She felt that she ought to try and keep Petra right away from the Home, and although this idea of visiting Mr Oakley was a step in the right direction, perhaps it wasn't a big enough step to keep Petra and Barry apart.

But Petra was a girl who thrived on attention from the opposite sex, and when she was introduced to Bob Oakley she began to radiate once more. Ann stayed for a few moments to help break the ice, but it was soon evident that her services were not required, and she felt a small pang of relief as she departed and went back to the private wing. Now she had to find out if Petra had made any sort of an impression on Barry during the afternoon.

Chapter Eleven

Barry seemed quiet when Ann returned to him. Her parents were doing the kitchen chores, and refused help from Ann when she went in to offer her services.

'Go and take care of Barry,' Mrs Bowman said softly. 'You won't get much chance of being alone with him today.'

'What's this?' Frank Bowman demanded. 'Have I been missing something around here?'

'Nothing, Father!' Ann said, backing hastily out of the kitchen, and she went into the sitting room to find Barry seated on the settee with one of the Sunday papers.

'Ann!' He looked up at her, and got to his feet as she approached him.

'Don't bother to get up, Barry,' she told him. 'You need to relax, you know. It seems to have been a strenuous week end, although I don't seem to have done much extra.'

'You were up at five,' he said, sitting

down again, and Ann joined him on the settee. She felt her pulses leap as their elbows touched, and she longed to push herself into his arms, but there was a strange feeling inside her that gave rise to much disquietness. It seemed to lie like a barrier across her tender feelings, and she had the uncanny feeling that Barry himself did not want to make contact.

'I've been up every morning at five this week,' she replied. 'I didn't feel tense until today.'

'Has it anything to do with Hugh Leighton?' he asked quietly.

'Hugh!' She frowned as she stared at him, and she found his blue eyes expressionless, his face taut but not strained, and she wondered what was passing through his mind. 'It has nothing to do with Hugh! What gave you that idea?'

'Well he's an old friend, isn't he? He's a very old friend!'

Ann moistened her lips, and she guessed that Petra had been talking about Hugh and the general situation.

'What do you think of Petra?' she countered. 'Did she keep you amused this afternoon? She does have that talent of being able to make amusing conversation.'

'She's a very nice girl,' he said thoughtfully. 'You have some very nice friends.'

'But you didn't get to meet Hugh!' She watched him closely, and he smiled.

'I did meet him when they arrived, before he came in to see you. Petra introduced us.'

Ann nodded, aware of the sort of things Petra might have said at the introduction. She tried to settle down at Barry's side, to get back into her normal loving frame of mind when they were together, but thoughts of Petra intruded upon her and she was held by a hostile feeling that would not permit her to relax.

'I was struck by Hugh Leighton,' Barry went on, talking more to himself than to Ann. 'He's a forceful character, isn't he?'

'He always was!' She shook her head slowly.

'He's in love with you!'

'He always has been!' Ann began to feel that she was a parrot, talking nonsense because it was all she had ever learned. She took a deep breath and half turned to face him, to bring the matter squarely into the open and tell him exactly what was in her mind, but the door opened at that time and Petra entered quickly.

Ann turned quickly at the sound of the door, and her heart seemed to cringe when she saw the girl. She took a deep breath and unconsciously moved away from Barry.

'You're soon back,' Barry said, getting to his feet and walking across to the fireplace.

'Yes. I chatted with Bob Oakley, but he's tired and needs to rest. However I've promised to come in and see him several evenings during the week.'

'We must make arrangements to pick you up,' Barry said instantly.

'I'm on night duty starting tomorrow night,' Ann said. 'I shall be able to pick you up, Petra.'

'I'll make my own arrangements for getting here and back if you like,' the girl said instantly.

'No. I won't hear of it,' Barry retorted. 'It's a great kindness you're doing for one of our patients, and the least we can do is see that you have no inconvenience getting to and from the Home.'

Petra nodded happily, and Ann suppressed a sigh. She felt as if everything was slightly out of focus. She couldn't account for the feeling, and sensed that Barry, too, was feeling differently about this situation. Had Petra managed to have some effect upon him already? Ann didn't know what to think, and she wished she could have put it all down to her imagination. Why should she think she might lose Barry? He had professed love for her, and that love ought to be strong enough to withstand any temptation that might be put in his way. If he couldn't resist temptation then his love was not strong enough and it would be better if they discovered it and parted.

The evening seemed to drag on. Ann did her best to maintain a cheerful manner, but her nerves were put sorely to the test. She could see that Barry was not in his usual mood, and that worried her further. She had to push her personal thoughts into the background and make an effort to keep them there, and all the time she watched the clock and wished the day was come to an end.

Eventually Petra glanced at her watch. The girl hadn't acted too outrageously in her contacts with Barry, but Ann's sensitive mind had been able to see the motives behind the girl's conversation.

'I think I've been here long enough,

don't you?' she demanded lightly. 'Poor Ann looks as if she'll fall asleep at any moment. You've been up since five this morning. You do have long days, don't you?'

'I'm getting used to them again,' Ann replied. 'But if you're ready to go then we'll drive you home.'

She was afraid that Barry might insist on taking the girl alone, but he nodded his approval at her words and got to his feet. Ann glanced at her watch again. The time was just after nine-thirty, and the day had seemed overlong to her mind. They left the Home, and Ann sat in the front seat of Barry's car as they went into town. Ann was feeling more tired by the minute, and she hardly heard what Petra was running on about during the short drive.

'You should have stayed at home,' Petra said when Barry had brought the car to a halt at the kerbside in front of Petra's flat.

Ann opened her eyes to find the girl leaning across the seat to look at her. 'Sorry!' she said slowly. 'The swaying of the car lulled me. What were you saying?'

'You ought to have gone to bed early

this evening,' Petra retorted. 'It's really too bad of me to take up your free time like I did. And I'm sorry Hugh had to leave as he did. It would have been more cosy with the four of us together.'

'Perhaps some other time,' Barry suggested.

'I hope so.' Petra opened the car door, and it was all Ann could do to suppress a loud sigh of relief. 'Goodnight! I'll telephone tomorrow evening about five and let you know if I can get away to visit Bob Oakley. Would one of you be prepared to pick me up?'

'Of course!' Barry spoke quickly. 'Just ring and ask for me and I'll see about it.'

Petra departed, and as the car door slammed behind her, Ann relaxed in her seat. Barry drove on, and Ann hoped the atmosphere which seemed to exist around them would shrivel up and die. She straightened in her seat and began to fight off her tiredness.

'Have you enjoyed your day, Barry?' she demanded.

'Well any friend of yours is a friend of mine,' he retorted.

'What does that mean?' She twisted in

her seat to look at his profile, and they were at the town limits, passing under the last of the street lamps.

'I found Petra a most entertaining girl!' His tones sounded a little odd to Ann, and she frowned. 'She is quite knowledgeable. I was surprised by some of her topics.'

'She had a very good education, as I did,' Ann pointed out.

'And we don't sit together and talk when we're alone,' he mused aloud. 'We don't get the chance to talk, do we?'

'We could if you wanted to!'

He chuckled, but it sounded strained, and Ann firmed her lips, still worried by the feelings inside her. She felt outraged in some obscure way. There was nothing tangible on which to pin the reasons for her mood. There was a sharp pain in her breast as if a dagger had been plunged there, and she considered that she had no feelings for Petra now. Was it jealousy? She had never been attacked by that green emotion before, but she sensed that it was causing the trouble now.

But why should she be jealous? Was it merely imagination that Barry seemed different since he'd shown Petra around the Home that afternoon? If he had fallen in love with Ann at first sight, wasn't it possible that he could do the same thing with Petra?

She was angry with herself for such thoughts, but she knew she was not imagining Barry's manner. He was different. He seemed to be brooding over something. But she would rather die than ask any questions, and she sat stiff and uncompromising while he drove back to the Home.

'You have had a long, exacting day,' he said. 'But you can have a lie in tomorrow morning. You don't have to get up. You're going on nights tomorrow.'

'It's a long time since I had night duty,' she replied. 'I am quite looking forward to it.'

They spoke in snatches, and there were longish silences between them. When they reached the Home Ann waited while he put the car away, and then they walked together to the rear entrance.

'There's another week end over,' he commented as they entered the building. 'I'm sorry it's come to an end. 'It's been most relaxing today.'

'I'm glad you've enjoyed it,' she responded.

He paused in the corridor and looked down into her intent face. Ann looked up at him, smiling faintly, and he nodded slowly.

'You do look tired. You'd better get to bed as soon as you can. I'll see you tomorrow. I expect you'll have a sleep tomorrow afternoon, won't you?'

'I shall have to!' She nodded. 'Goodnight, Barry!'

'Goodnight!' He smiled and turned away without kissing her, and Ann stared after him in shock and surprise. For a moment she felt that the world had come to a standstill. Then she caught her breath while her heart beat fiercely in protest. She turned very quickly and hurried into the private wing before he could turn around to see her, and there was hot panic in her breast as she went to her room.

She was hurt! She felt as if she had been slighted. She began to think all manner of things, and her mind was filled with confusion as she prepared to go to bed. But she felt too tired to worry about anything, and as soon as she crawled thankfully into her bed she lost herself in slumber ...

Next morning she awoke with a headache, and was surprised to find that the

236

time was almost nine-thirty. She arose and dressed leisurely, her mind heavy with dread, and she was relieved to find her mother was on duty. She didn't feel like talking to anyone at this time. She had a frugal breakfast and then wandered around the private wing like a caged tigress, her mind working coldly and with great precision.

She could remember almost everything that had been said the previous day, and she searched each item of conversation in search of anything that might prove to be significant. But she dearly wished she knew exactly what lay in Barry's mind. It hadn't been her imagination that he had seemed to change during Petra's visit. The fact that he had omitted to kiss her goodnight proved that he had something on his mind. And she was afraid to probe for it in case she discovered something she wouldn't like!

Feeling stifled by the atmosphere which seemed to pervade the wing, Ann put on her coat and went out, to walk the path down to Clover Farm. She smiled wryly when she reached the brook and stood for a moment on the little bridge. All her dreams had blossomed from the moment she reached this spot upon her return home. Now something seemed to have gone wrong, and she sensed it keenly.

Perhaps Barry was having second thoughts. Perhaps he was unsettled by the swiftness of their coming together, and she frowned as she remembered the way he had seemed out of sorts over his previous engagement. Perhaps he was not the marrying type. It could be that his natural desires had carried to the point of thinking about the future, where marriage logically waited, and perhaps he was beginning to shy at the idea. Had it happened to him before? She had no way of knowing, and she went on with her mind dimmed by the blackness of her thoughts.

She didn't see Barry before going to sleep that afternoon. She lay down at two and slept through until six-thirty, rising tiredly to dress and think of spending a few hours with Barry. She was trying subconsciously to straighten her mental attitude. She had fallen so deeply in love with Barry that she seemed unable to maintain a fair balance. Her dreams had been smashed once before, and now she was jerking away from the prospect of a repetition of the same situation. It was a purely automatic defensive reflex, but it caused her great disquiet.

Ann found her mother in the sitting room when she went through from her bedroom, and Mrs Bowman got immediately to her feet.

'Hello, Ann, did you have a good sleep?' she demanded.

'Fine thank you!' Ann smiled, determined to maintain a normal manner. She didn't want anyone asking pointed questions.

'I'll get you something to eat.' Mrs Bowman started towards the door.

'No, I'll get it,' Ann replied. 'You sit down again, Mother. I'm not very hungry.'

'All right, dear! Barry called in about thirty minutes ago. Petra had telephoned him to say she'd like to come out this evening to visit Mr Oakley, and as you were still asleep he's gone to fetch her.'

Ann didn't like the sound of that, and she had to fight down her sense of jealousy. She made a desperate effort to keep her expression blank, and was aware that her mother was watching her closely. 'It's good of Petra to give up her time like that,' Ann said.

'Yes, she's always led a very full life, hasn't she? From what I've heard about her she never has a spare moment.'

Ann was thinking that usually Petra had a selfish motive whenever she exerted herself, and this time the girl's motivation was Barry. She turned away to go to the kitchen for a meal, and Mrs Bowman called to her as she reached the door of the room.

'Are you worried about anything, Ann?'

'Worried? No! Why do you ask?' Ann faced her mother and regarded her with steady gaze.

'It just passed through my mind. You'd talk things over with me if you had any problems, wouldn't you?'

'I'd come to you immediately if I needed advice,' Ann said readily, and she smiled.

'Good!' Mrs Bowman was satisfied, and Ann went on her way.

Barry appeared by the time Ann finished her meal, and he stood in the doorway of the kitchen and regarded her with intent gaze. Ann didn't realize he was there until he spoke, and his voice startled her.

'Hello, Ann! Did you see Hugh?'

'Hugh?' She turned to look at him, wondering what he was talking about.

'Petra told me he was coming here to see you this evening.'

'How would Petra know that?'

'I don't know. I suppose she's as friendly with Hugh as you are.'

'But I'm not at all friendly with him,' she retorted. 'Is there something on your mind, Barry?'

'No! Why?' He tilted his head to one side as he regarded her.

'I can't help wondering, that's all.' She suppressed a sigh as she took off her apron. 'Why would Hugh come here to see me?'

'Because he's in love with you!' Barry shrugged a shoulder. 'That could be a reason. I'd want to come and see you if I were away from you.'

She nodded slowly. 'I told Hugh yesterday that there was no hope for him!'

'So he did tell you of his love! I thought there was something on your mind all yesterday evening.'

Ann smiled faintly. There had been something on her mind, but Hugh hadn't been to blame for it. She felt her small resentment against the situation of yesterday crumbling away, and suddenly her stiffness was gone and she wanted to throw herself into his arms. She caught her breath as the feeling persisted, and took a step towards him. Then she remembered that he hadn't kissed her goodnight and that he'd seemed to have changed his manner since yesterday afternoon. She resisted her desires and stood watching him. He looked into her eyes, and his own were hard and narrowed.

'I've been thinking about us,' he said slowly.

'Really?' She tried to sound carefree, but failed miserably, and her tones quivered and almost cracked.

'We've plunged into love, haven't we?' He tried to smile, but his lips merely thinned against his teeth. 'I think we made a mistake! We shouldn't have taken everything for granted so quickly. I think your feelings stemmed from the fact that you were disappointed in love, and I needed an excuse to get free of my previous engagement. We were thrown together and we really are merely strangers. I think we should have a cooling off period, Ann, so we can find out what really does lie in our minds.'

She stared at him silently, wishing she could know exactly what lay in his mind, and she found his eyes expressionless, his face devoid of emotion. He was obviously waiting for her to agree with him, and she stifled her feelings and nodded slowly.

'I expect you're right,' she said, and there was a picture of Petra in her mind. She had sensed from the very first moment the girl had suggested coming to the Home that something like this might happen, and she had been powerless to prevent it. So much for Fate taking a hand in her life! She smiled slowly, watching his face for expression. He seemed relieved at her words, and she held her breath for a moment, feeling little remorse because her dreams were cracking before her very eyes.

'We didn't let anyone know that we were going around together,' Barry went on. 'So there'll be no explanations to make. We can still see each other, of course, and if you want me to take you out any evening you've only got to say the word.'

'I was beginning to go out too often, as a matter of fact,' she said. 'I'm not a girl like that by nature, you know.'

He nodded, smiling, although it seemed a little forced. 'Well I'd better get on duty,' he said. 'I promised to relieve your father for the rest of the evening. Would you take Petra back to town when she's ready to go?'

'Certainly. I'll watch for her when visiting is over.' Ann remained motionless, her legs paralysed for the moment, and Barry nodded slowly then turned away. He left silently, and as the door closed behind him, Ann sighed bitterly.

So that was that! The thought passed through her mind, but she was still too dazed to accept it or feel pain. She blinked as she considered. What had happened? Was Petra at the bottom of it all? Ann did not know what to think.

She was still standing in the kitchen when her mother came in to see what she was doing. Ann made a stupendous effort to appear normal, and she smiled as she met her mother's gaze.

'I've just finished clearing away,' she said. 'Now I'd better see if Petra is ready to go back to town.'

'I'm going out with your father for a couple of hours,' Mrs Bowman said. 'See you when we get back.'

'I go on duty at ten, so you'll know where to find me if you want me.'

Mrs Bowman nodded and departed, and

Ann paced the sitting room while she tried to control her confusion. Time passed her by, and she was greatly surprised when there was a knock at the door. Going in answer to open it, she found Petra standing there, a wide smile on her pretty face.

'Hello, Ann. Barry told me you'd be driving me back to town. Am I too early for you?'

'No. Come in, Petra. How did you get along with Mr Oakley?

'He likes me fine! We get along very well together. But then I always managed to get along well with the opposite sex.' Petra seemed on top of the world. 'I'm very glad I came here yesterday. Just think what I would have missed if I hadn't asked. I wouldn't have met Barry for a start.'

Ann noticed the girl was using Barry's name, and that was just another sign that her world had been turned upside down in the past twenty-four hours.

'We'd better start out to take you home because I go on duty at ten,' Ann said carefully.

'I never cease to admire you!' Petra said as they left the private wing. 'How do you cope with your work? I wouldn't know where to start in this place.'

'It's all a matter of training,' Ann replied.

When they were in her car and driving towards Wentham, Ann felt the desire to question Petra about her feelings towards Barry, but she didn't. She felt that she couldn't take the news that Petra had fallen in love with her own fateful lover! But Petra loved to talk, and she chatted incessantly on the short drive. Ann was left in no doubt that Petra found Barry most charming and attractive, and that seemed to be the end of the situation. When Petra liked somebody as much as she liked Barry then nothing was permitted to stand in her way, and that was the impression Ann gained by the time she had delivered the girl safely to her own door.

'See you again, Ann,' Petra called cheerfully. 'Am I glad you came home from abroad! Look what I would have missed if you hadn't returned.'

'Goodnight,' Ann replied lightly, and she drove away with the certain knowledge that if she hadn't come home again to seek refuge she would have saved herself a lot of grief. It seemed to be a prime case of rushing blindly into worse trouble than she left behind.

Chapter Twelve

Days passed in blind succession during the next week because Ann was on night duty and working to a routine that was completely the opposite to everything she knew. But nothing she did would ease the ache in her heart. She could not see Barry off duty because he seemed to be working when she was free, and when they did chance to meet around the Home he didn't have much to say for himself. He had lost that easy familiarity of his, and seemed to be in the kind of mood that had held him during her first few days at home, when he had been still engaged to his previous fiancee.

The few words they had together were mainly about duty, and at no time did he offer to take her out for the evening before her duty began. It seemed as if he had withdrawn completely from the frame of mind which admitted to love.

Ann was lonely and hurt by what had happened. She couldn't begin to understand how it had come about. Petra was coming to the Home every other evening to visit Bob Oakley, but it was obvious that the girl really came to see Barry. On two occasions, Barry drove Petra home after her visit, and didn't return to the Home until very much later.

By the next week end she had become so hurt by the whole affair that she took herself off in the Fiat to try and find some diversion in town. It was Saturday afternoon, and the weather was dull but fine. She kept well away from Petra's flat, and went to do some shopping for necessities. But her mind was not on what she was buying and she found no pleasure looking in the shop windows. She started back to the car park, and walked into Hugh Leighton.

'Ann!' His gloomy expression was chased away by a smile of pleasure. 'This is a surprise! Been doing your shopping?'

'Just a few odds and ends.' She was pleased to see him, for beneath her own unhappiness there was a strand of worry concerning him. A pang struck through her as she told herself that he loved her, and she firmed her lips as she began to move on. A restlessness gripped her and

248

she could not stand still.

'What's the hurry?' he demanded, placing a hand upon her arm. 'You don't have to run off like that, you know. We are old friends. Come and have a cup of tea with me. I'm at a loose end, and it looks like being a very long week end.'

Ann hesitated. She felt so lonely that the chance to talk to someone was not to be lightly discarded. She could imagine that he was feeling exactly how she felt and she wouldn't wish it on anyone.

'Come on,' he insisted. You don't think I'm going to bite you, do you?'

'All right. I do have some time on my hands,' she admitted.

'You're going to meet the new boyfriend later, are you?'

'What new boyfriend?' She frowned as she looked into his dark eyes.

'You told me last week you were in love with someone else. That is the truth, is it? You're not just putting me off!'

'I'll come and have tea with you if you promise not to discuss any matter pertaining to last week or your feelings or mine,' she said.

'That's a deal!' He took her shopping bag and then held her elbow, and they walked along the pavement to a crowded tea shop.

Ann had misgivings almost as soon as they sat down, for she saw Petra and another girl seated at a corner table. They didn't look up from their animated conversation, and Ann sat with her back to them, hoping against hope that they would not look across. Hugh didn't spot them, either, and he waited for a waitress to come by, chatting desultorily the while.

'I'm sorry about last Sunday,' Ann said slowly.

'I thought we were not going to discuss it?'

'I just want you to know that I am sorry for being so sharp. You paid me a great compliment with your admission, and I didn't act very graciously.'

'I imagined that you were under great pressures last week end,' he said.

'I was, and I didn't want any complication on the scene. Do you forgive me, Hugh?'

'Of course I do!' He smiled and reached across the table to take hold of her hand. 'You can do no wrong, Ann, in my eyes. I want you to know that!'

She nodded, feeling sorry for him as

well as for herself. Their tea came and she poured it. He thanked her, then sat looking down into the steaming brown liquid, his thoughts hard pressed. She watched him intently, noting his grim expression, and she wished there was some way she could help him. They drank their tea, and chatted generally, but neither of them had their minds upon what they were saying. Then a hand fell upon Ann's shoulder, and Petra was exclaiming loudly in her ear.

'Ann! Hugh! This is a surprise! I never expected to see you two together!'

'We just dropped in for some tea!' Hugh said.

'What a pity you didn't come earlier, or saw me over there in the corner.' Petra beamed at them, her eyes alight with pleasure. 'I can't stay now. I've left my assistant in charge of the shop, and she's not responsible enough for the job. See you again. I shall be going out to the Home this evening, Ann. Shall I see you there?'

'No,' Ann said quickly, and a wave of bitterness swept through her. 'I'm not going back early. It's my day off, and I don't want to set eyes on the Home until I really have to go back.'

'Goodbye then!' Petra smiled at them both and went on her way, leaving her companion at the corner table.

'She's a strange girl,' Hugh said after Petra had gone. He leaned his elbows upon the table and cupped his chin in his hands. 'At one time I thought I was in love with Petra.'

'Then you decided you liked me better and that was the end of Petra's hopes,' Ann said softly.

'And I've loved you ever since!' He was silent for a moment, his face composed. 'But I'm getting over it now, I think. This past week has been hard, but the daylight is beginning to seep through the solid parts of my head. I know I can't have you now and I'm trying to make my subconscious mind accept it. But I don't think I shall ever stop loving you, Ann.'

'What about this girl in York?' she demanded.

'She isn't a patch on you!' he declared. 'But I might marry her at that.'

'Don't marry her if you don't love her,' Ann warned. 'That would be the worst thing you could do. Don't be that kind of a fool, Hugh!'

'It's difficult to know what to do for the best,' he went on.

Ann didn't mind discussing the situation now, for she sensed that he would no longer try to push his love into her face. He had come to realize there was no chance for him, and she was glad, for it meant his troubles were practically over. But then she thought of Barry and Petra, and her mind went whirling off at a tangent again.

'Will you come out with me for the evening?' he asked suddenly. 'You said you weren't going back to the Home. I've got the feeling that you're upset at something, and if there's anything I can do then you've only got to say the word.'

'There's nothing wrong,' she replied. 'I'd like to have your company for an evening, Hugh. But I'm afraid that if I do spend some time with you then you'll begin to think there's a chance for you.'

'I promise that I won't think anything at all, and I certainly won't broach it,' he said. 'I tried to push you into loving me but that didn't work.' He smiled ruefully. 'I'm never going to forget last Sunday. But that's in the past. I'm hoping to see you now and again and that the sight of me sometimes will instil some sort of feelings into you. If you do fall in love with me then all well and good, but I'm not going to push it, Ann. That would only make trouble for the both of us.'

She nodded slowly, and sighed as she agreed. 'All right. On those conditions I'll spend the evening with you. I don't feel like going back to the Home, and there's no fun being alone.'

'This is what friends are for,' he said eagerly. 'What would you like to do this evening?'

'I'm not really in the mood for anything!' She smiled slowly. 'I'll be rather poor company, I'm afraid.'

'Something has upset you!' He fixed her with a keen stare, and Ann shook her head slowly. 'I know you well enough, Ann, to see when you are upset.'

'Well it's nothing I want to talk about, Hugh,' she told him.

He nodded sympathetically, and they prepared to leave the cafe. Ann really didn't feel in the mood for anything except being in Barry's company, and she wished she could have turned the clock back to the previous Saturday! That was when it had all started.

She could not get rid of her unsettled

feeling, and during the evening she tried hard to give her full attention to Hugh. He was most considerate, and didn't once broach the subject that obviously lay very close to his heart, and she enjoyed herself as much as was possible.

But when they parted in town, Hugh took her hands and held them tightly. His face was set harshly and his eyes gleamed in the street lighting.

'Ann, if you ever need anyone to turn to then think of me,' he said. 'I'll always be around where you're concerned.'

'It's very good of you, Hugh but I can stand on my own two feet.'

'Perhaps so, but there may come a time when you'll need someone, and it might be a help if you know you can turn your head in my direction. You have only to crook your little finger and I'll come running'

She smiled as she thanked him, and his sincerity touched her. But she left him and drove homeward, her mind filled with doubt and hopelessness. There had to be some way in which she could put her mind to rights, she thought grimly. How was it that a man could make a girl's life so miserable, and just by not doing anything?

When she put the car away she stood in the shadows for some moments, just lost in thought and thinking of nothing in particular. She was miserable, and there was nothing she could do about it. The next day she was off duty, and there was nothing she could look forward to. If only Barry had asked her out, or something! She smiled thinly as she walked towards the rear door of the Home, and her tears were not very far away.

A movement near the back door alerted her and she frowned as she peered into the shadows. She saw a figure standing on the path, and hesitated as she tried to identify it.

'It's only me, Ann.' Barry spoke quietly, and her heart seemed to miss a beat at the sound of his voice.

'Barry!' His name was like a prayer on her lips, and she stifled the quivering sigh that emanated from her lips. 'What on earth are you doing out here at this time of the night?'

'Just getting a breath of fresh air,' he retorted.

'A breath of cold air,' she said, trying to sound light hearted. 'You're on duty, aren't you?'

'Yes. I've just made a round. Have you had a nice evening? You didn't come back for tea. Petra was here and she said she saw you in town.'

'I had a nice time!' Her voice tried to trail off, but Ann forced herself to sound cheerful.

'You're on day-off tomorrow! I expect you're going out for the day!'

'I am!' She didn't know what made her lie, but she knew she could not let him see that she was hurt in any way. It was natural to lick wounds in private, and there was a thread of pain running through her mind. She didn't doubt that he would be going out with Petra. He would be off duty, and the knowledge that only a week ago would have found them making plans to go out together cut through her mind like a surgical saw.

'Well have a nice time!' He stepped aside for her to enter the house, and she knew he wanted to go on his way.

Ann passed him and entered the house, and she didn't turn or wait for him to follow. She firmed her lips and walked towards the front stairs.

'Goodnight, Barry,' she said brightly.

'Goodnight,' he acknowledged.

Ann looked round when she reached the stairs, and she was surprised to find that Barry had disappeared. He hadn't even followed her along the corridor, and she knew he was taking the back stairs to his quarters. He didn't even want to prolong his stay in her company now. The knowledge twisted her heart, and she went on to her room and hastily threw herself into bed.

But there was no slumber for her at first. She could not contain all the misery that floated in her mind. There was a picture of Barry in the forefront of her thoughts, and one of Hugh in the background. Her mind revolved sickeningly, and she wished she could find a solution to the situation. If she were merely a nurse here, with no family ties, she could have put everything right by leaving and losing herself among strangers. But she had only just returned home and she couldn't go away again without causing her parents at least a lot of pain. She was trapped here and there was nothing she could do to help herself.

Sleep eventually came to her aid, and she slumbered until morning, when she awoke and lay with her mind returning to the thoughts that had occupied her the night before.

Ann realized that she could not go on in this way, but there seemed nothing for it but to tolerate the situation. She felt heavy minded and listless, and although the day was hers she had no desire to go out or seek any kind of enjoyment. When she arose and dressed she had no idea what to do with herself, and the day seemed to stretch ahead of her like a jail sentence.

At breakfast she sat at the table with her parents, and her father was reading his newspaper. Mrs Bowman made low conversation, not wanting to attract her husband's attention. But Ann would not be drawn, and it was all she could do to keep her expression clear and her voice normal. There was a quivering misery inside her that threatened to betray her to the worst of her emotions, and she had no wish to break down and lose control of herself before her parents.

'What are you going to do with yourself today, Ann?' her mother enquired at length.

'I'm going out for the day!' Ann remembered what she had told Barry, and although she was wishing that she hadn't mentioned it, she was aware that it would be better to pretend she was going out for the day. She didn't want Barry to think she was hurt at losing him. If he wanted Petra then he could have the girl, and he wouldn't even know that Ann was suffering a broken heart.

'Where are you going?' Interest sharpened Mrs Bowman's tones.

'I don't know yet,' Ann replied cautiously.

'Are you going with Barry?'

'No.' Ann paused for a moment, thinking quickly. She didn't want her parents to know there was something wrong with her life. 'I'm going with Hugh. I spent last evening in his company, and he wanted me to go with him today.'

'Oh!' Mrs Bowman sounded a little bit surprised. 'You were out with Hugh last evening! Are you getting interested in him now?'

'We've always been great friends, Mother!' Ann countered.

She left the table soon after, excusing herself with the reason that she had to get ready to go out. When she reached her room she sighed heavily, because the last thing she wanted to do was go out for the day. But she had committed herself and there was nothing for it but to go through with it.

She was ready to leave at ten-thirty, and she went out to the garage, to find rain falling heavily, and her heart almost failed her when she saw Barry in the other garage, cleaning his car. He looked up at her as she approached, and his face seemed set with a stern expression.

'Not a nice day for it,' he remarked.

'For what?' she asked.

'For your day out.'

'How did you know I was going out for the day?'

'Your mother told me.' He didn't look at her for a moment, but when he did his eyes were averted from hers.

'You're off duty today! Aren't you going out?' she asked.

'I expect I shall later on, if the rain stops. I hope it gets out fine for you.'

'Thank you!' Ann unlocked the garage door and went inside to open the Fiat. She drove out, and Barry came forward to close the garage door for her. She nodded her acknowledgement and drove on, looking at him in the driving mirror as she pulled away. He went straight back to cleaning his car.

She drove steadily, and didn't know where she was going! But she entered the town and parked in the centre, leaving the car and walking around the shops, looking in at the windows but hardly seeing anything. The rain came down harder and she stood in a doorway, waiting stoically for the weather to ease. It wasn't until a voice exclaimed at her back that she turned to find Petra standing behind her, and she looked round in amazement because she was at Petra's shop.

'What on earth are you doing here?' Petra demanded.

'Just window shopping, and I didn't realize this was your shop, Petra.'

'I thought you were miles away by now.' The girl came to Ann's side and looked into her face. 'Is anything wrong? You don't seem very happy.'

'I'm all right! I was deep in thought, that's all. Where are you going now?'

'Out to the Home! It's Sunday and visitors are permitted all day, remember.'

'Of course!' Ann smiled. 'How are you getting out there?'

'Barry will be along for me very shortly.'

Petra looked at her watch. 'I rang him a few minutes ago to check that we had arranged for him to pick me up. I've got an errand to do before he arrives, so you will excuse me, won't you?'

'Certainly!' Ann forced a smile. 'Off you go! I'll see you later. I'm just gazing in the shops. I came into town earlier than I intended.'

'Goodbye then! Have a nice time!' Petra smiled and hurried away along the pavement.

Ann stared after the girl, her eyes showing a reflective mood. All this had happened in a week! One short week! She firmed her lips as she considered. Why had she been shown a glimpse of heaven with Barry if they had been fated to part? Whoever had said it was far better to meet and part than never to meet at all had it all wrong. She was firmly convinced of that.

She went on walking, unmindful of the rain, and she was quite soaked by the time she returned to her car. Sitting in the vehicle, Ann wondered what to do with her time. She was lost in her misery, and time was her greatest enemy. She couldn't return to the Home and admit that she had lied about her day out or even suggest that something had gone wrong with her plans. She would have to stay away until evening, then return to lie about the good time she'd had!

It was almost lunch time, and she was hungry. She considered going to a restaurant for a meal, but decided against it. There were too many people in town who knew her, and she didn't want any word of her doings getting back to the Home. Her low spirits gradually sank lower, and she realized that unless she made a great effort to snap out of her mood she might never find the strength to do so. But she couldn't summon up the determination she needed.

While she sat in the car deliberating, her eyes were idly scanning her surroundings, and when she saw Hugh's car entering the park she cringed, for she didn't feel in the mood for chatting to anyone. She started the car, waiting until Hugh had pulled to the end of the line, then drove out quickly, wanting to get away from all human contact.

She drove for a long time, her mind just ticking over in misery. There was a dullness inside her that would not be denied, and it seemed to be eating her very soul.

How she got through the day, Ann couldn't clearly recollect later. She drove all the time, and rain smeared down, isolating her from everything material. She followed a road that never ended, and as dusk came she realized with a great sense of surprise that she had travelled in a wide circle and was approaching Clover House from the opposite direction. But she didn't feel like going in because she was quite unable to face anyone she knew. Her mother would ask a lot of interested questions, and Ann was at a loss to answer in a satisfactory manner.

She turned off at the village and followed the minor road to Clover Farm, and when she reached the clustered buildings night had fallen. Driving into the yard, Ann took a deep breath as she alighted, and she walked unsteadily to the front door. Charles Bowman appeared in answer to her knock, and he stared at her in surprise.

'Ann! Is something wrong?'

'No, Uncle! Should there be? Can't I come and see you without you thinking the end of the world has come?'

He chuckled, and she smiled, losing

some of the remoteness which had held her in its grip all day.

'Come in,' he said, and opened the door wide. 'I suppose you had nothing better to do so you found your way here.'

'Now you know that's not true,' she retorted, crossing the threshold. 'I haven't been home long, but I've come to see you several times. Is Paul at home?'

'No! I'm all alone! Paul is courting strongly now! I don't see much of him at all these days when he's finished working. Have you come for the evening?'

'If you can put up with me,' she replied.

'I was just sitting down to tea. Have you eaten?'

'I haven't! I'll join you if I may.'

'Come along then! I could do with some company. Let's do things in style!'

Ann nodded as she tried to enter into his mood. He was always cheerful, she thought, and yet he'd had a lot to grieve over. But he hadn't given way. He had known that life went on no matter what happened, and she felt a little better as she considered. If she could take a leaf from his book she would survive. She actually began to cheer up as he led her into the big farmhouse kitchen!

Chapter Thirteen

Ann spent a quiet evening with her uncle, and some of his fatalistic calm seemed to attach itself to her mind, so that by the time she took her leave she was feeling easier deep inside. Charles Bowman walked to the car with her.

'Thanks for dropping in, Ann! I've enjoyed your company,' he said. 'It's a lonely life when one's offspring grows up and begins to make its own way in life. But your parents realize that better than I. You've been away three years!'

Ann nodded. 'That's the way it goes, Uncle.'

'I'm a stay at home myself!' He smiled. 'I'd be quite happy if I never had to leave the farm. But then we're not all alike. How are you settling down now you're back? Are you missing those foreign climes?'

'Not at all! I'm beginning to feel as if I've never been away!' Ann stared ahead for a moment, her thoughts racing. It was quite true! Gerry had quickly left her mind, and if Barry hadn't stepped right into his place then there would be no clouds at all upon her horizon. She smiled as she looked into her uncle's face. 'Well thank you again for such a pleasant evening, Uncle. I'll come over and sit with you soon. I'm on the two till ten shift next week, so my evenings are spoken for.'

'Goodbye then, Ann, and don't work too hard!' Charles Bowman stepped back and waved a hand as Ann started the car.

She smiled and waved, then drove off, and she was relieved to find that the blackness of mind which had occupied her all day was now back in perspective. She drove home, and was thoughtful as she parked the car. The garages were locked, and she alighted to try and open them. When she failed she left the car with the lights on and hurried into the Home to find out what had happened to the keys.

Mrs Bowman was in the sitting room of the private wing, and she looked up eagerly when she saw Ann. Now Ann could face her mother without fear of the questions that would be flung at her, but she spoke first, forestalling her mother.

'Have you any idea where the garage keys are?' Ann asked.

'Barry had them. Have you left the Fiat outside the garage?'

'Yes!' Ann nodded slowly.

'Well leave it there and Barry will put it away when he comes in. He took Petra home earlier. If the garages are locked then Barry has taken the keys with him. He always puts the car away for me. Now come and sit down here and tell me about your day!'

'I'm a bit damp, Mother. We walked in the rain and I got wet. I'd better go and change before I catch cold. I'll take a shower, then go straight to bed. I'm very tired.'

'You've been with Hugh all day?' her mother demanded.

'No!' Ann was warned by the older woman's expression. She turned cold as she imagined that perhaps Hugh had called her during the day. She hadn't considered that possibility when she'd lied about her activities.

'Oh! I thought you were going out with Hugh!' Mrs Bowman studied Ann intently.

'I had arranged to do so, but I pulled out at the last moment. He's been getting too friendly of late, and I thought it better to let him know that there's no hope for him as far as I'm concerned.'

'I see!' Mrs Bowman nodded. 'It's better to avoid complications where you can. But you've also broken with Barry, haven't you?'

'There was never anything between us that needed breaking off,' Ann retorted quickly. 'Don't jump to conclusions, Mother.'

'Sorry, I wasn't meaning to.' Mrs Bowman nodded slowly. 'I think you'd better hurry and take off your wet clothes. When you've taken your shower I'll bring you a mug of hot milk.'

'Thank you!' Ann forced a smile and turned away. She paused in the doorway and looked back at her mother, who was still staring at her. 'Are you sure it will be all right about the car? It is unlocked and in the open.'

'It will be all right. Barry will put it away when he gets in.'

Ann nodded and departed, and she sighed heavily as she went to her room. She was telling herself that she would have to be very careful in future! She didn't want anyone to know the truth. It might seem absurd to everyone that she had come home and fallen in love with Barry at first sight. If it had worked out all right then it wouldn't have mattered. But now he was seeing a lot of Petra then her own feelings had to be kept secret. She knew her mother had practically guessed at the truth, but she felt that she could fool her if nothing else came up to reveal the truth.

After a shower she was more than ready to go to bed, and she was almost asleep when Mrs Bowman came into the room with a mug of hot milk on a tray.

'Come and drink this, Ann,' her mother said gently, sitting down on the foot of the bed.

'Thank you!' Ann sat up and blinked away her sleepiness. She took the mug and sipped from it, keeping her eyes averted from her mother's face.

'I don't want you to think that I'm prying, Ann, but where have you been today?'

'I told you this morning, I went out for the day!'

'I had the impression you were going with Hugh!'

'That was my original plan, but I changed it. I went for a drive during the day, and came back to Clover Farm and spent the evening with Uncle Charles. He was all alone.'

'I see!' Some of the worry left Mrs Bowman's face. 'I've been wondering about you ever since Hugh telephoned.'

'You can forget about Hugh, Mother. I shan't be going out with him again.'

'And what about Barry?'

'What about him?'

'You'd fallen in love with him, hadn't you?'

'No! We were attracted to one another. I'll admit that, but it didn't go any further.'

'That's a great pity. I began to have hopes about you and Barry.'

Ann forced a smile and then drank her milk. She handed the mug back to her mother and settled herself in bed once more. Mrs Bowman tucked her in, then bent to kiss her forehead.

'Goodnight, dear. See you in the morning.'

'Goodnight, Mother.' Ann closed her eyes resolutely, and she was almost asleep by the time Mrs Bowman closed the bedroom door ...

Next morning after she'd had breakfast,

Ann wondered what she could do. She was filled with a new sense of resolution. She was not going to permit anything to upset her life. If Barry didn't want her then that was the end of it. She wasn't going to sit down and weep. She was made of sterner stuff, and she'd go on about her daily duties as if nothing had ever gone wrong. She decided to go out for a walk across the fields, and a glance from the window warned her the weather was wet. But that didn't daunt her and she began to dress accordingly

The telephone rang as she put on her raincoat, and she compressed her lips as she studied the instrument before lifting the receiver. Then she spoke, and heard Hugh's voice at the end. She had suspected it was Hugh, and she suppressed a sigh. She was in no mood for any kind of arguing.

'Ann, I haven't been able to sleep a wink all night,' Hugh said instantly.

'What's wrong?' she demanded.

'When I rang to talk to you yesterday your mother told me we were supposed to be out together for the day. At first I didn't get it, but I worked it out afterwards that you were using me as an alibi. What's going on? What are you up to? What sort of a man is this chap you've fallen in love with? Why can't your mother know who he is?'

'I'm sorry, Hugh, but it was convenient to use your name. I have no excuses. We were out together the evening before, and I didn't think it would do any harm using you as an excuse.'

'I don't mind, as far as it goes. But are you all right? Is anything wrong? Can I help in any way?'

'No thanks. I appreciate your offer, but nothing is wrong.'

'I don't see why you had to lie about us!'

'I can't explain it. Will you forgive me for using your name?'

'Of course! But yesterday I went to York to see this girl I'm supposed to be engaged to, and I made it official. I know I'm never going to have you, so I've got to make do with what I can get. I think I can make a go of it, so I'm announcing wedding plans, the date, everything.'

'Congratulations!' Ann felt her mind lighten considerably at the news. That was one aspect of her worries removed, at any rate. 'But are you sure you're doing the right thing?'

'Reasonably.' He chuckled harshly. 'I'm not going to mope around for something I know I can never have. I wish you luck with this unknown man of yours, and I hope one day to be able to meet him. I'm curious to see what kind of man you finally picked for yourself. I can't stay and chat with you because I'm pushed for time this morning. So long as you're sure there's nothing I can do for you! Only I've been worried about you. There's a lot I don't understand.'

'Well you don't have to worry. Everything is under control, Hugh. Thank you for calling. You're very thoughtful.'

'Being thoughtful has never got me anywhere,' he declared with a chuckle. 'Now I must go. But this seems to be the time of year for wedding plans. I heard this morning that Petra is going to get married in a month.'

'Petra!' Ann was thunderstruck. 'Where did you hear that, Hugh?'

'One of the crowd! It was arranged yesterday, I believe. Anyway, perhaps you'll be the third one! Goodbye!'

The line went dead before Ann could

275

reply, and she stood with the receiver in her hand and listened blankly to the purring sound. A sigh escaped her as she replaced the instrument upon its rest, and then she walked to the door, firming her lips and struggling against her thoughts.

It hadn't taken Petra long to hook Barry! The knowledge was cold and dismal inside her, no matter how she tried to remain cheerful. And Barry! He didn't know his own mind. He'd been engaged three weeks ago, but that was broken off. Then he had professed love for Ann, and now Petra was on the scene, and it looked as if Petra had snatched the prize. But could she hold what she had won?

She paused by the door and glanced back at the telephone. For a moment she toyed with the idea of ringing Petra to offer her congratulations. They had always been friends, and Petra hadn't known that Ann herself was interested in Barry. The girl had done nothing underhand. But Ann knew she could not talk about it right now. In a day or two, or when she saw the girl again would do.

Leaving the Home, Ann started towards the garages, but paused when she saw Barry at one of them. She stared at him for a moment. It would be easy to congratulate Petra, but Barry was another matter. She had told him she was in love with him, and he wouldn't forget that. He was the only one who knew, and he would be aware that she was suffering.

A wave of emotion gushed through her and she turned away, wanting to hide herself. If Clover House hadn't been her home she would have rushed back inside and packed her bags and fled. But she couldn't go. She had to stand firm and face this without emotion. It would need all her courage and strength, but she had to do it for her own peace of mind.

She took the long way round to the path, and skirted the garages and escaped unseen, although she spotted Barry several times through the trees. She examined herself and discovered that her distress was not too great. It was there and it hurt, but she could control it. No one would ever know what she was feeling. It was her deep secret and it would stay with her.

Her mind seemed to take flight as she walked across the fields. Rain fell steadily, but she did not notice it. The day was dull, and it seemed to match her mood.

This was a perfect day for musing about Life! She thought of Petra, and the way the girl had come up on the scene and taken Barry. But what was ordained was ordained. She smiled slowly as the thought crossed her mind.

She crossed the bridge, and did not pause to think of that first day when she had met Barry here. She didn't dare let her thoughts dwell upon it. That was an incident she would do well to forget. Barry had not been intended for her, and the sooner she accepted the fact the better. Had she taken to him on the rebound? Could she have fallen in love with a stranger so quickly and completely? It didn't seem feasible now, and she tried to convince herself that it had been all a dream.

When she passed the farm she watched out for sign of her uncle or Paul, and she didn't want to see either. The rain eased as she continued, and before many minutes had passed there was a break in the clouds and a weak but determined sun began to thrust gentle rays towards the earth. Ann smiled as she glanced skywards. If only her troubles could pass as quickly as rain clouds!

She came upon a narrow lane, and turned from the fields and walked along it, knowing exactly where it would lead her. She took a deep breath and walked on resolutely, swinging her arms and trying to make her mind match the speed of her legs. She could beat this thing! She would beat it!

There was a junction in the lane, where a smaller cart track cut across it, and Ann turned right and began to follow the track. It was muddy and she could not make such fast time. The slower pace seemed to give her thoughts a better chance of working against her, and for some moments she suffered as she struggled to beat her mind.

The track petered out, as she knew it would, when it reached a copse, and Ann paused and looked around. She was alone in a damp world, and her misery seemed to be gaining the upper hand over her. Despite her resolution she could not stem the flood of despair, and she sighed bitterly as she felt herself losing the small amount of ground which she'd thought she had won.

A movement along the track caught her attention and she frowned as she half turned to see who was there. This was

Clover Farm land, and for a moment she thought her cousin Paul was coming towards her. Then her heart gave a great leap, and she felt her legs trembling as she recognized Barry.

Ann stood quite still as he came towards her, and she pictured him as she had seen him last, at work in the garage. How had he managed to follow her here, and what was he doing here?

'Hello!' He spoke rather sharply as he came up. 'I saw you when you left, and you made it quite obvious that you didn't want to speak to me.'

'I didn't think you had seen me!' she faltered. She thrust her hands into the pockets of her raincoat and clenched them to stop the trembling that was running through her. She watched his face with intent brown eyes, and her congratulations trembled on her lips. But she couldn't force herself to utter them.

'May I walk the rest of the way with you?' he demanded.

'I'm making for home now,' she said, and walked on slowly, feeling the old sensations of love and hope beginning to rise up in her mind. She thought of the last time they had walked this way together, and a sob came to her throat, although she managed to stifle it and turn it into a cough.

'Are you catching cold?' he demanded. 'I've never met a girl quite like you before, Ann. You're never happy unless you're out walking in this kind of weather. Any normal girl is quite content to sit by the fire, but you've got to drag yourself out, and you're not content to take a short stroll. You've got to make it a cross-country hike each time.'

'Well you don't have to share that sort of thing with me any longer,' she retorted, immediately on the defensive. 'We all have our strange ways. What about you, for instance?'

'What about me?' He stared at her for a moment, and she held his gaze for a few seconds, then looked away. His blue eyes were sharp and bright, and she had to fight the desire to push herself into his arms. 'Well, what about me?' he demanded.

'It doesn't matter!' She shook her head and continued walking.

'Nothing matters any more!' His voice was harsh. 'I wish you had never come home from the Caribbean!'

'Me too!' Her voice quivered. 'I wouldn't

have met you then!'

'I thought my life had become straight-forward when you came on the scene.' He glanced at her, and Ann met his gaze and tried to stare him out.

'Well I'm not to blame for the unhappiness that's come about.'

'What do you mean?' He halted and looked down at her, and Ann felt like a schoolgirl confronted by an angry master as she watched him.

'I understand congratulations are in order! I heard about it in a roundabout way!'

'Congratulations?' There was a frown on his face.

'Petra is going to be a bride!' Ann spoke softly.

'So I heard!' He smiled thinly. 'And you're the one who brought it all about. If you hadn't brought her to the Home last Sunday week it would never have happened.'

'You don't have to tell me. I've thought of nothing else since it happened.' Her voice quivered again, and she feared she might break down and cry.

'It was a bad Sunday all round.' Barry shook his head. 'Everything was going so well! I thought Fate had planned for us to be together for the rest of our lives. But it wasn't to be. That's obvious now.'

'Only too obvious,' she agreed. 'I hope you'll be very happy, Barry.' She stumbled over his name, and her lips quivered. 'If you're happy then everything is all right.'

'Me?' He was looking at her with narrowed blue eyes, and Ann had to fight the impulse to start running away from him.

'You're the one who's getting married!'

'Me?' he said again, and a look of bewilderment crossed his face. 'What on earth are you talking about?'

'You and Petra!' She paused and looked him squarely in the eyes.

'What about me and Petra?' he demanded in dangerously even tones.

'You're getting married!'

A silence followed her words, and Ann looked into his face and tried to concentrate.

'I'm marrying Petra?' he asked. 'Where did you hear that?' He shook his head slowly. 'What's going on here? Is this some kind of a crazy conversation? How can I be marrying Petra when Bob Oakley proposed to her last night and she accepted him?'

'Bob Oakley?' Ann reached out her hands and grasped his arms, and she swayed as the whole world seemed to whirl about her. 'Not you?' she demanded, gripping him tightly.

'How did I get into this?' he asked softly. 'I'm in love with you, but since Sunday week when Petra came to the Home everything has been different. She told me that Hugh was madly in love with you and had been for years, and she said you were in love with Hugh. That's why I dropped out of the scene. I had to give you the chance to make up your mind about the situation. You started going around with Hugh and I didn't get the chance to see you at all during the past week. You were out with him on Saturday, and again all day yesterday. I realized that I'd lost you, and that's that. But now you tell me I'm due to marry Petra. What's on your mind, Ann? I just can't follow you any more.'

She laughed tremulously, and for some moments she felt that she had taken leave of her senses. He shook her gently, a questioning light in his pale blue eyes.

'All I know is that I'm not in love with Hugh and that I love you,' she retorted.

'That's how it was when I first came home, and nothing has happened to change the situation. I had the chance to love and marry Hugh years ago if I'd wanted him. But he never was the right man for me.'

'And you thought I lost interest in you when Petra came on scene!' His eyes began to show signs of his awareness. 'You never let her know that you loved me, did you?'

'I didn't!' Ann shook her head, and tears were beginning to gather in her dark eyes. She moistened her lips, and the next instant Barry had taken her into his arms.

'Of all the foolish things!' He looked down into her face, shaking his head slowly, and then he kissed her.

Ann clung to him with all her strength, and now her tears were rolling down her cheeks. But nothing mattered. Her mind was repeating that Barry still loved her, and the misery of the past week boiled up inside her and burned itself out.

'I told you I loved you, Ann,' he said softly, looking at her. 'I meant it when I first told you and I'll always mean it. I love you. I don't profess to understand what's been happening this past week, but explanations can wait. Just tell me that you still love me. That's all I want to hear.'

'I love you, Barry!'

'That's it! Now dry those tears and let's get back to the Home. I want everyone in the place to know about this. I'm tired of keeping such great news a secret, and once we've told everyone there'll be less chance of misunderstandings.'

He kissed her again, and they stood exposed to the elements. Rain was hissing down but they didn't notice. Ann clung to the man she loved and her tears of joy mingled with the rain drops. But now everything was all right, and she had the feeling that nothing would ever come between them again. They seemed welded together as they continued their embrace, and Ann could only think that this seemed to be the time of year for people to announce weddings!

'I love you, Ann!' Barry told her repeatedly, and the words seemed to stick in her heart as they strolled through the rain, back towards Clover House.

It was like the beginning again, Ann thought happily, this time there would be no misunderstandings. They both knew without doubt that they were really in love ...

This Large Print Book for the Partially sighted, who cannot read normal print, is published under the auspices of

THE ULVERSCROFT FOUNDATION

THE ULVERSCROFT FOUNDATION

. . . we hope that you have enjoyed this Large Print Book. Please think for a moment about those people who have worse eyesight problems than you . . . and are unable to even read or enjoy Large Print, without great difficulty.

You can help them by sending a donation, large or small to:

**The Ulverscroft Foundation,
1, The Green, Bradgate Road,
Anstey, Leicestershire, LE7 7FU,
England.**
or request a copy of our brochure for more details.

The Foundation will use all your help to assist those people who are handicapped by various sight problems and need special attention.

Thank you very much for your help.